A DOOMED FERRY RIDE . . .

Denny withdrew a short black gun, not much bigger than Matt's water pistol, and pointed it at Bonnie.

Bonnie stared at the gun. She didn't know what kind it was, only that it was aimed at her heart. A small gun could be just as deadly as a large one. Fear crashed against her like ocean waves.

Denny wouldn't get away with it; Bonnie was positive of that. As soon as Denny shot her, Matt would scream and run upstairs for help—and what would Denny do then? Shoot Matt, too?

ABDUCTION!

ABDUCTION!

PEG KEHRET

SCHOLASTIC INC.
New York   Toronto   London   Auckland
Sydney   Mexico City   New Delhi   Hong Kong

No part of this publication may be reproduced, stored in a retrieval system, or transmitted in any form or by any means, electronic, mechanical, photocopying, recording, or otherwise, without written permission of the publisher. For information regarding permission, write to Puffin Books, a division of Penguin Young Readers Group, a member of Penguin Group (USA) Inc., 345 Hudson Street, New York, NY 10014,

ISBN 978-0-545-26028-2

Copyright © 2004 by Peg Kehret. All rights reserved. Published by Scholastic Inc., 557 Broadway, New York, NY 10012, by arrangement with Puffin Books, a division of Penguin Young Readers Group, a member of Penguin Group (USA) Inc. SCHOLASTIC and associated logos are trademarks and/or registered trademarks of Scholastic Inc.

12 11   14 15/0

Printed in the U.S.A.   40

First Scholastic printing, April 2010

Lexile is a registered trademark of MetaMetrics, Inc.

For my daughter, Anne Konen,
love always

ABDUCTION!

CHAPTER 1

Denny Thurman stuck the black wig on his head, pulling it snug above his ears. He put on the brown shirt with the fake UPS logo, buttoned it over his T-shirt, and tucked it into his brown pants. Last he pressed a false mustache on his upper lip, pushing hard to make it stick.

He smiled at himself in the mirror. His own mother wouldn't recognize him.

The temporary rose tattoo on his left biceps showed below his sleeve, but the slight bulge of the handgun in his shoulder holster was barely noticeable under his shirt.

Denny hurried downstairs to his car, feeling nearly as excited as he did when he placed a bet. An hour later, he stopped the car in the alley behind his ex-wife's house and put on thin plastic gloves. He got out but left the engine running, in case he needed to drive away quickly. He looked both ways, saw no one, and walked to the gate that connected the garage to the fence.

He reached over the top of the gate, feeling for a latch. Good. No lock. He opened the gate and stepped into the yard. One hand rested in his pants pocket, the fingers wrapped around a small plastic bag containing a piece of broiled steak. With luck, the dog would come to him without the bribe. If that happened, Denny would have a steak sandwich for dinner tonight.

He wished he could remember the dog's name, but Denny had never paid attention to the dog—he didn't care for animals—and six years was a long time. By now it might be a different dog.

Denny's eyes swept across the small yard: neatly mowed grass, a swing set, sunbursts of yellow tulips in full bloom, a bird feeder and birdbath. No dog, though. Surely Anita would have a dog; she had been crazy about dogs, and so had Bonnie. They both petted every mutt they met, acting as if each was the grand champion of all time. Anita even kept dog biscuits and a leash in the car, in case she saw a stray in need of help.

The dog must be inside. Denny would have to pry open a door or window. He hoped the house wasn't wired with an alarm system.

Denny walked toward the house but stopped before he reached the screen door. His eyes swung to the corner of the house, to a metal flap at ground level. A dog door! If he could coax the dog out the door, he wouldn't have to break in, after all, and wouldn't risk setting off an alarm.

Denny stood outside the dog door and whistled. "Here, dog," he called. "Come get your steak." He whistled again.

When no dog appeared, Denny pulled off a piece of the steak, pushed the door flap inward, and tossed the meat inside.

Soon the flap pushed outward, and an elderly black-and-white terrier waddled out. The once-dark muzzle was gray, and the dog walked stiff-legged, as if his knees didn't bend well anymore. It's the same dog, Denny thought. He must be over one hundred in dog years by now. Denny wondered if the dog would remember him.

"Hey, dog," Denny said.

The dog blinked, looking around as if unsure where the sound had come from. He's almost blind, Denny realized.

Denny held the steak toward the old terrier. The dog sniffed, wagged his tail, and came closer. When he tried to take the meat in his teeth, Denny pulled it away. He put the steak back in the bag and shoved it into his pocket. He had the dog; why waste the steak?

He removed the leash from his other pocket, looped it around the dog's neck, and tugging gently, led him out the gate. The dog followed willingly but couldn't jump into the car; Denny had to lift him into the backseat.

Before he shut the door, he unbuckled the dog's collar and read the ID tag. *Pookie,* it said, then a phone number. That's right; Pookie. Denny remembered now. Foolish name for a dog. The ID tag clinked against a rabies tag and a King County dog license as Denny tossed the collar into the weeds beside the alley.

He opened the driver's door and slid behind the wheel. He glanced at himself in the rearview mirror, to be sure the wig and mustache were still in place. Satisfied with his appearance, he drove slowly out of the alley and headed for the school, removing the gloves as he drove.

The dog whined and pawed at the back of Denny's seat.

"Too late to cry," Denny said. "You're the bait now, Pookie, my boy. You're the insurance to make sure Matt gets in the car without calling for help."

CHAPTER 2

Bonnie hadn't thought about the dream in years, which was fine with her.

She remembered it when her best friend, Nancy, said, "Last night I dreamed I jumped out the window during math, landed in the ocean, and rode off on a sea turtle."

"I can never recall my dreams," Bonnie said as she pulled on her Mountain Middle School shorts and T-shirt for PE class. "Except for one. I used to have it a lot."

"You had the same dream more than once? Mine are different every night."

"This one was a nightmare. The first time I had it was the night my dad died."

7

"What was it about?"

Bonnie leaned down to tie her shoes, surprised by the chill she felt. "It's hard to explain."

"Try me."

"In the dream I'm lost on a huge prairie, acres and acres of grass higher than my head. I spend the whole dream running, calling out for help that never comes."

"Just grass? No vicious lion chases you? You don't fall into a pit full of poisonous snakes?"

"I know it doesn't sound scary, but whenever I had the dream I always woke up crying, with my heart pounding." Each time she had felt as if a heavy black fog hung over her bed, seeping through the blankets into her skin and making it impossible ever to feel happy again. Bonnie shuddered, remembering.

"You were four when your dad died, right?" Nancy said.

"Right. The thing is, I didn't know about death until it happened. I'd heard the word, but I didn't think it had anything to do with me. I never expected it to happen to my family, to my daddy."

"Most four-year-olds wouldn't."

"My grandma tried to help me understand, but she made me more scared than before."

"What did she say?" Nancy asked.

"She told me, 'Everyone dies, but usually not until they're very old.' She meant to comfort me, but I thought Daddy was old. When you're four, twenty-six seems ancient."

"Small wonder you had nightmares."

The girls left the locker room and began jogging around the gym with their classmates.

"Grandma talked about heaven and angels and how it was a tragic accident," Bonnie said, "but I focused on, *Everyone dies*. Everyone included my mother, who was the same age as Daddy. That night, I dreamed I was lost on the prairie."

"You were afraid you'd be an orphan."

Bonnie spoke softly. "I've never told anyone about the dream before. Mom used to come into my room when I'd wake up crying, and she'd ask what I had dreamed, but I always pretended I couldn't remember. At first I was superstitious about it, afraid if I told the dream it would come true. Later I worried there was something wrong with me for having the same bad dream over and over. I didn't tell Mom because I didn't want to go to the doctor. I was scared I'd get a shot."

"You don't need a master's degree in psychology to figure out that nightmare," Nancy said. "It's the classic fear-of-loss dream. You lost your dad, and you were afraid your mom would die, too. Perfectly normal. They'd march you straight to a kiddie shrink if you *didn't* have dreams like that when a parent died. Do you still have it?"

"No. I had it a lot at first, and then it gradually came less often. It stopped when I was eight or nine."

"So you are now a well-adjusted thirteen-year-old who has overcome a terrible loss and gotten on with her life. No more nightmares."

"You, on the other hand," Bonnie said, "are a serious mental case who secretly yearns to escape from school and ride away on a sea turtle."

"You got that right," Nancy said.

Although Bonnie smiled, the familiar cold ache settled in her stomach. It didn't happen often anymore. To be honest, whole weeks went past when she never thought about her dad at all, but when she did think of him she felt as if she had a hole in her heart, like some vital piece of herself was missing.

Remembering how suddenly she had lost him always made her feel vulnerable. If tragedy could knock on her door without warning once, it could arrive again.

She wished she hadn't told Nancy about the dream. Now she felt anxious and edgy, as if some unexpected disaster were about to strike her family.

You're being paranoid, Bonnie told herself. Mom's at work; Matt's in kindergarten; Pookie's probably asleep in a patch of sunshine on the rug. It's an ordinary morning, and everybody's safe. Still, the vague feeling of dread stayed with her.

CHAPTER 3

It had been simple for Denny to learn Matt's room number. After he found Anita's address in the telephone directory, he called the school district office and asked which school kids in that area would attend. Next he had called the school and said he was Matthew Sholter's uncle.

"I want to send balloons to his classroom on his birthday," Denny had said, "but I don't know which room he's in."

The student who had answered the phone looked up Matthew Sholter and then told Denny everything he needed to know, including what time all-day kindergarten started and let out, and where Room 27 was located. She called the boy Matt, rather than Matthew. Useful information.

Jefferson School sat on the corner of Milton Street and Seventh, a sprawling one-story structure that had overflowed its quota of children years ago and now depended on portable buildings to house the extra students.

For the last three days, Denny had parked in front of the school every afternoon, in the line of cars that arrived to pick up children who spilled out the doors like popcorn from a popper promptly at two thirty-six.

Until now Denny had left the school by himself. Today he would have a passenger.

Denny glanced at the car's clock. Two twenty-three. He was right on schedule.

The first day Denny had wondered how he would know which one was Matt. It seemed impossible that he wouldn't know his own son, but one kid looked pretty much like the next to Denny, and he'd never actually met Matt or even seen any pictures of him. He hadn't wanted to, until recently.

Maybe the kid resembled him. Tim and Thomas, Denny's nephews, looked a lot like Denny's brother-in-law, Winston, so Matt would probably look like

Denny. The boy might be a real chip off the old block, Denny had thought, and I'll know him the second I see him.

He had watched the children rush outside, but none of them seemed even slightly familiar. Maybe Matt was absent. As Denny watched the children line up for the school buses, or head to the waiting cars, he saw Bonnie join a small blond boy in the second bus line.

Denny hadn't seen Bonnie since the divorce, but she had been six or seven during his brief marriage to her mother, so he recognized her instantly. She was taller, of course, and more slender, but she still had thick, curly brown hair and a lopsided smile. The boy showed Bonnie a drawing, and she gave him a thumbs-up.

Denny stared at the boy with Bonnie. He wore a Donald Duck T-shirt and jeans. That must be him, Denny thought. That's Matt. My son.

The same scene repeated the next day, and the next, as Denny parked near the school, watched for Matt, and made his plans.

After the second day, Denny knew which boy was Matt, even before Bonnie came.

Matt always arrived first and got in line. Then Bonnie dashed across the playground and rode home with him. The trick would be to coax Matt into the car quickly, without alarming the bus driver or the other kids, and drive away before Bonnie got there. He planned to wait outside Room 27 and intercept Matt the second he emerged.

Denny had come back to the school one night and walked around, deciding where to park so that he wouldn't be seen by the other parents or the bus drivers. That's when he saw the notice on the front door: ALL SCHOOL VISITORS MUST SIGN IN AT THE OFFICE AND GET A VISITOR'S BADGE.

He couldn't take a chance on being stopped for not wearing a badge, but he didn't want to sign in, either.

Denny had soon figured out what to do.

Now he was finally putting his plan into motion. He had rehearsed the whole thing in his mind so many times that when he began to do it for real, he felt as if he were merely repeating actions he had already taken.

Instead of parking where the parents lined up, he stopped on the side street, close to the door Matt always came out. He opened the trunk of his car, then took out a clipboard and a cardboard box addressed to the school library. Carrying the box under one arm, he walked around to the front entrance, past the flagpole, and into the school office.

"UPS," he said to the woman behind the counter. "I have a delivery for the library."

The woman glanced at his brown uniform. "You

need to sign in, please," she said, "and wear a visitor's badge. The library is down the hall, on your left."

Denny scrawled UPS on the sign-in ledger, thanked the woman, hung a badge around his neck, and walked out of the office. Instead of heading for the library, he went straight for the door at the end of the hall, the one next to Room 27.

Then something happened that Denny had not planned for—a lucky break he had never imagined as he mentally rehearsed this day's activity.

The door of Room 27 opened, and Matt stepped into the hallway. He closed the door behind him and headed straight toward Denny.

"Matt," Denny said.

"I'm going to the bathroom," Matt said. He held a piece of yellow paper toward Denny. "I have a hall pass."

"I was coming to get you out of class," Denny said. "You're supposed to come with me. Right now."

The boy shook his head, frowning.

"It's an emergency," Denny said. "Pookie got hurt, and I'm taking him to the vet. Your mom wants you to go along so Pookie won't be so scared."

Matt's eyes grew wide. "Pookie's hurt?"

"He got hit by a car. I stopped to help, and when I called the number on Pookie's tag, your mom asked me to get you and then take Pookie to the vet. She's going to meet us there." Denny held out his hand to Matt. "We have to hurry!"

Matt shook his head again, putting his own hands behind his back. "I don't know you," he said. He took a step backward. "I'm not supposed to go anywhere with someone I don't know."

"You're right to be cautious," Denny said. "It shows you're a smart kid. But I checked in at the office; see my visitor's badge? That's how I knew where to find you. If you walk outside with me, you can see my car from the playground. You'll see I'm helping Pookie."

Denny went out the door, holding it open for Matt.

Matt followed Denny out the door to the playground.

Denny pointed. "That's my car," he said. "Pookie's in the backseat."

Matt looked toward the green sedan. He saw the dog's nose pressed against the side window of the man's car.

"Pookie!" Matt said. "How bad is he hurt? Are his legs broken? Is he all bloody? Is he going to die?"

"He might, if we don't get him to the vet right away. Pookie's scared. He needs you to ride along to the vet, so he won't be afraid." He extended his hand again.

Matt hesitated, glanced again at the dog, took the man's hand.

Together they ran across the playground toward the street.

While the boy climbed in beside the dog, Denny tossed the box and the clipboard into the trunk, his heart thumping in triumph. His plan had worked perfectly. The woman in the school office never suspected that a fake UPS logo had been stitched on last night by Denny himself. Matt had seen the dog in the car and left the school without a whimper.

As Matt hugged Pookie in the backseat, Denny started the engine and drove away, being careful to stay within the speed limit. The last thing he needed was to get pulled over for a traffic violation.

He rounded the corner as the first school bus pulled into the drive. The car clock said 2:34.

CHAPTER 4

By the time Bonnie got to her last class of the day, her mood had brightened. Friday afternoons always felt full of promise, even if she had no special plans for the weekend.

As she finished her math assignment, Nancy slipped her a note.

Can you leave baby brother with your neighbor and go to the mall with Sharon and me after school? Mom's driving us. We're going to try on shoes and get free makeup samples.

Bonnie sighed. She would love to go shopping with Nancy and her sister, but she wasn't supposed to ask Mrs. Watson, her neighbor, to watch Matt unless it was an emergency. She wrote *I have to stay with Matt. Lucky me. Bring me some samples—my face needs all the help it can get.* She passed the note back to Nancy.

Bonnie often wished she had an older sister instead of a younger brother. Sharon helped Nancy with homework and hairstyles, taught her the latest dances, and let Nancy listen to her CDs. Best of all, Nancy never had to be in charge of anyone but herself.

Last year, in sixth grade, Bonnie and Nancy often hung out together after school. They'd go to the library or talk with their friends for a little while before they walked home. Matt was in day care then, and Mom picked him up after work, so Bonnie didn't have to worry about him.

This year, with Matt in all-day kindergarten, Bonnie had to hurry from the middle school to the adjoining elementary school as soon as the final bell rang. She rode the bus home with Matt and took care of him until Mom arrived.

Bonnie knew it was important to watch Matt after school; she knew she saved Mom a lot of money each month. She also knew it was a pain.

Matt always wanted to practice pitching a baseball, with Bonnie as the catcher. If she didn't catch for him, Matt threw a tennis ball against the garage door for hours at a time. *Thwack! Thwack! Thwack!* Each *thwack* left a faint, round green spot from the tennis ball's fuzz. The Sholters had the only house in town with a polka-dot garage door.

The final bell rang at two thirty-six. Bonnie could never figure out why it wasn't two-thirty or two forty-five. An example of adults setting rules that don't make sense.

Bonnie slipped her backpack on and hurried toward the school library. She had two books due and didn't want to owe a fine. After dropping the books off, she headed across the ball field toward Matt's school.

She arrived as the lines of students began boarding the yellow school buses. Her eyes darted from front to back of the second bus line, but she didn't see Matt. She went to the bus door and called in to the driver, "Is Matt already on the bus?"

"Haven't seen him," the driver replied.

Bonnie frowned. Wouldn't you know it. The one day she didn't come straight to the bus, Matt wasn't there. Maybe he had stayed after school to help Mrs. Jules.

She rushed to Room 27. Mrs. Jules was pinning new material on a bulletin board.

"Do you know where Matt is?" Bonnie asked. "He isn't in the bus line."

"He got a hall pass to go to the bathroom a few minutes before school got out. I let him leave because he said he couldn't wait and when he didn't come back to class, I assumed he went straight to the bus."

"He isn't there," Bonnie said.

"I'll look in the boys' restroom," Mrs. Jules said. "Sometimes Matt stands in front of the mirror pretending he's pitching a baseball, and he forgets the time."

Bonnie nodded. Matt did that at home, too. It drove her nuts when she was waiting to use the bathroom herself.

Mrs. Jules cracked the restroom door and called, "Anybody in there?" When there was no answer, she went in. Seconds later she came out. "He isn't there. Let's check the bus again."

This time Bonnie boarded the bus, looking at all the passengers. Matt wasn't there. As soon as she got off, the doors wheezed shut. The first bus in line pulled out of the school driveway; Bonnie's bus followed.

"You check the playground," Mrs. Jules said. "I'm going to the office to alert Mr. Quinn."

Bonnie nodded. She rushed to the playground and looked at the monkey bars, the ball field, and the basketball court. No Matt.

She ran to the office where Mr. Quinn, the principal, was speaking over the public-address system, alerting all teachers that Matt Sholter had not boarded his bus.

"If you see Matt," Mr. Quinn said into the microphone, "bring him to the office immediately." He clicked off the mike and turned to Bonnie. "Has he ever done this before?" he asked.

Bonnie shook her head, no. "Once he was late because he goofed around with his friends, but Mom scolded him, and since then Matt has always gone straight to the bus. He gets there before I do."

"Maybe he went home with a friend today, and your mother forgot to tell you."

"Mom would never forget," Bonnie said. "She always makes sure we know what we're supposed to do after school."

"Let's call her, to be sure," Mr. Quinn said. "Do you know her work number?"

Bonnie gave it. Her insides felt hollow as she listened to Mr. Quinn ask for Mrs. Sholter. A few seconds later, he identified himself and said, "Matt didn't get on the school bus today and we can't find him. Did he go home with a friend?"

He talked another minute or so. When he hung up, he said, "She's on her way. Matt was supposed to go home as usual."

"I don't like this," Mrs. Jules said.

Apprehension crawled up Bonnie's arms and across the back of her neck.

"Let's not panic yet," Mr. Quinn said. "I've had situations before where a youngster gets in trouble at school and doesn't want to go home, or they get invited to play at a friend's house and forget to call. Sometimes, especially with the kindergartners, they get on the wrong bus. Then they have to ride the whole route before they're brought back here. One student fell asleep on the bus and wasn't found until the driver had already parked in the bus barn."

Bonnie could easily have disputed each of Mr. Quinn's theories. Matt never got in trouble at school, and he wasn't allowed to go anywhere with a friend unless Mom had arranged it. Certainly he wouldn't have boarded the wrong bus; they had ridden bus number two all year. She didn't argue with the principal, though. It was Mr. Quinn's first year at this school, so he didn't know Bonnie. She knew he was only trying to make everyone feel more optimistic.

While Bonnie looked out the office window, hoping to see Matt approach, Mr. Quinn called each of the bus drivers.

Matt was not on any of the busses.

The black fog of Bonnie's old dream seemed to hover at the edge of the school yard.

CHAPTER 5

Puppy kisses! Puppy kisses!" Matt said.

The old dog, wriggling with happiness, slurped the boy's face.

How disgusting, Denny thought as he watched in the rearview mirror. He had never understood why some people act as if their dogs were part of the family. Besides getting unsanitary slobber on the kid's face, the mutt was probably shedding all over the backseat.

"Pookie doesn't act hurt," Matt said. "Are you sure he got hit by a car?"

"He feels better because you're here," Denny said. He stuck two fingers inside the wig and scratched his scalp. It was too warm to have an extra head of hair.

"Why are you going this way?" Matt asked. "Pookie's vet isn't this way."

"We aren't taking him to the vet. You said the dog is okay."

"Then where are we going?"

"Home."

"Home isn't this way, either."

"I know where I'm going," Denny said. "This is a shortcut." He glanced in the rearview mirror again. The boy stared back, one hand fingering his earlobe.

The boy's nervous, Denny thought. I need to put him at ease, but how?

Denny had no idea what to say. He didn't know anything about kids. What should he talk about? He tried to think how Celia and Winston handled their boys.

Denny leaned over, opened the glove compartment, and felt inside. He picked up a large chocolate bar and tossed it into the backseat.

"Here you go," he said. "Something to munch on."

"I'm not allowed to eat chocolate," Matt said.

"You are now."

"Really?"

"Yep. When you're with me, I make the rules and I say every kid needs some chocolate now and then. Go ahead. Take a bite."

"Won't I get hives?"

"Hives? From a candy bar? No way."

Matt ripped the wrapper open and took a bite. "Yum," he said. "It's good." He took another bite.

Pookie whined.

"Pookie wants some," Matt said.

"So give him a piece."

"Mom says chocolate is bad for dogs."

"Well, that shows how much she doesn't know. Would you want to eat nothing but dog food all the time?"

"No."

"Neither does Pookie."

Matt broke off a piece of chocolate and gave it to Pookie, who swallowed it whole and immediately begged for more.

"He likes it," Matt said. "So do I."

"Of course you do. Everybody likes chocolate. Chocolate is one of life's great pleasures."

"Want a bite?" Matt asked.

"No, thanks. I had my own candy bar a little while ago." Denny smiled, congratulating himself for thinking of the candy.

Imagine a kid who never eats chocolate bars.

Anita had always worried too much about health.

Once when he'd given Bonnie a sip of his beer, Anita acted as if he'd tried to poison the girl.

As he drove, Denny glanced frequently at Matt, who continued to share the chocolate bar with the dog. Denny felt no surge of fatherly affection, no pride because this handsome boy was his son. He felt only relief that he had succeeded in getting Matt away from the school without being questioned.

Although he'd been prepared to use his gun if a teacher had tried to stop him, he was glad it hadn't been necessary. A school shooting would have brought every cop in the county swarming toward the scene; a kid who didn't go home after school would attract far less attention. No one had seen him take Matt; he would not be connected to the missing boy.

"I need to go to the bathroom," Matt said.

"We'll be home soon."

"I have to go really bad. I was on my way to the bathroom when I met you, remember?"

Denny tried to think of a safe place to stop. He didn't want someone to notice the dog and the kid, and then remember later what kind of car they were in. "You'll have to wait," he said.

"I can't. I'm going to wet my pants."

"Hold it! I'll find a place."

"Could we stop at McDonald's to use the bath-room?" Matt asked. "Mom does sometimes."

"I'll stop at Marymoor Park. It has a public bath-room." People walk their dogs around Marymoor all the time; nobody would pay attention if Denny stopped there.

A loud retching sound came from the backseat.

"Pookie's going to throw up," Matt said.

Denny slammed on the brakes and pulled the car on to the shoulder, but before he could get stopped, Pookie gave back the chocolate he'd eaten.

"Yuck," Matt said. "Pookie barfed all over the seat."

Denny swore. "Keep the dog on the floor," he said as he pulled back on to the road and continued toward Marymoor.

"It stinks in here," Matt said. "I think I'm going to be sick, too."

"No! Roll your window down and breathe the fresh air."

Matt put the window down and stuck his face in the breeze while Denny drove into Marymoor Park, ignored the parking-fee sign, and stopped near a play-ground.

Three empty cars waited in the parking lot. Denny parked as far from them as he could. He didn't think

Anita would have reported Matt missing yet, but he was taking no chances. The fewer people who saw Matt with him, the better.

"You go to the bathroom," Denny said. "I'll clean up the mess."

Matt ran up the sidewalk to the restrooms.

The leash still hung from Pookie's neck. Denny lifted the dog to the ground, then led him to a large sign that gave park regulations. After making sure no one was watching, Denny wound the end of the leash around one of the wooden signposts and tied it with a double knot. Pookie sat beside the post.

Denny went into the men's room, grabbed a fistful of paper towels, and held some of them under the faucet. He could hear Matt singing inside one of the stalls. "Come straight to the car when you're done," he said.

"Okay."

As Denny started out of the building, a trio of young women emerged from the women's restroom. Talking and laughing, they paid no attention to Denny as they walked toward their car, but he lingered next to the building until they drove away before he returned to his own car.

Denny cleaned up the seat and threw the towels in a trash can. He removed the school's visitor badge from around his neck and tossed it in the trash, along with the gloves. He unbuttoned the brown shirt and discarded it, then yanked off the wig and the false mustache and stuffed them in the trash. He added the clipboard, but the empty box didn't fit; he put it back in the car.

He had wondered where to get rid of his disguise. This park was perfect—a public spot, well used. Soon other people would dump their litter bags and toss their empty coffee cups and even put soiled diapers into that same trash can. When it got emptied, nobody would sort through the contents. It would all go straight into the garbage truck, and there would be no evidence that Denny Thurman had ever been here.

Denny got back in the car, eager to leave. He could hardly wait to see Winston. For years, his brother-in-law had showed off his two boys.

The last time they'd been together, Winston had suggested Denny had no children because he never stayed married long enough to father a child. "You'll never have kids," Winston had said, "because your wives file for divorce on the honeymoon."

Furious, Denny had determined to find his own kid and prove Winston wrong.

It had been easy to learn Anita had given birth to a boy. The library offered old newspaper records on microfiche, and he knew approximately when the baby would have been born.

He read all the birth announcements for that month and quickly found the notice for Matthew Lee Sholter.

A week after he read the birth notice, Denny moved to a bigger apartment and made plans to take the boy to live with him. He would laugh in Winston's face and claim he had known about his son all along.

Denny knew Anita would never give Matt up, not even for a visit. There was no point asking her. If he did, it would tip her off that he wanted Matt, and then he'd be a prime suspect when Matt disappeared. The only way to get his son was to abduct him.

Tomorrow Denny would see his sister and brother-in-law and their boys. They lived on Bainbridge Island, in a house near the beach. Winston and Celia frequently invited him to join them for a weekend, but Denny usually made up excuses not to go. The two noisy kids got on his nerves, and Winston's endless bragging about the little monsters irritated him.

Even worse, Celia always tried to change Denny's lifestyle. Once she had dragged him to a doctor, and now she nagged him constantly to take the medication the doctor had prescribed.

She didn't know the doctor had also recommended Denny start counseling and take an anger-management class. Well, forget that. Denny didn't need some stuffed shirt with a string of medical degrees messing with his head. He'd thrown the pills away and refused to see the doctor again.

This time he looked forward to seeing his sister and her husband. This time Matt would be with him. Celia might even be too shocked to nag.

Denny started the engine. What was taking the kid so long in there?

A flatbed truck with some heavy equipment on it pulled into the parking lot, and a burly man jumped down.

Denny tapped his fingers on the steering wheel impatiently. He had hoped Matt would be out of the men's room before anyone else went in.

The truck driver walked along the side of his rig, checking the tie-downs.

Come on, Matt, Denny thought. Get out here!

The truck driver jogged off down the path, without looking at Denny. When he reached the sign where Pookie was tied, he gave the dog a pat and kept going.

Finally Matt came out and headed toward Denny's car. Denny opened the front door on the passenger's side. "Sit up here with me," he said. "It doesn't smell as strong."

Matt climbed into the front seat and buckled his seat belt.

He looked at Denny and gasped. "You changed your hair," he said, "and you shaved off your mustache." One hand nervously fingered his earlobe. "You're wearing a new shirt, too."

"Smart kid. Very observant."

"You look a lot different."

"Do you think I look like you?" Denny asked as he backed out of the parking space.

"No."

"Do you know who I am?"

Matt shook his head no.

"I'm your dad."

Matt's eyes narrowed. He examined Denny for a few seconds, then asked, "What's your name?"

"Don't you know your own dad's name?"

"I know it. My mom told me."

"My name's Denny Thurman."

"Oh."

Denny could tell Matt recognized the name.

"You had on a wig before, didn't you?"

Denny didn't answer.

An uneasy feeling crept over Matt as he thought about everything this man had told him. Something was wrong here, and as soon as he got home, he'd tell Mom exactly what had happened.

Denny left the parking lot and headed out of Marymoor Park toward Highway 520. He glanced once in the rearview mirror, but he couldn't see the dog.

Good-bye, Pookie, he thought. Good riddance.

CHAPTER 6

It had been less than ten minutes since the school buses left, but it seemed like forever to Bonnie. *Where was Matt?*

"Who are Matt's friends?" Mr. Quinn asked.

Bonnie and Mrs. Jules named four children from Matt's class. Mr. Quinn called each of their homes. Twice he got an answering machine and left an urgent message. The other two times, a woman answered, questioned her child, then reported the child hadn't seen Matt after school let out.

"Maybe someone gave him a ride home today," Mr. Quinn said. "Perhaps a neighbor or somebody else Matt knows saw him in the bus line and offered to drop him off. Maybe he's home right now, waiting for you."

Bonnie called her own number, although she knew Matt wouldn't be there. They always rode the bus home together unless Mom made other arrangements in advance. Always.

The answering machine clicked on. "Matt," Bonnie said, "if you are home, call the school right away." She read the number off the telephone base.

Bonnie hoped her mom would get there soon.

"Did Matt have a problem today?" Mr. Quinn asked Mrs. Jules. "Did you send a note home?"

Mrs. Jules said, "He didn't get in trouble in class. He rarely does. Matt's one of my easiest boys, except for his tendency to think about baseball too much."

Something's happened to him, Bonnie thought. Maybe the anxious feeling that started in PE hadn't been because of remembering the dream; maybe it was a premonition.

Was Matt going to disappear from her life without even a chance to say good-bye, the way her dad did?

Mr. Quinn turned to the school secretary, Mrs. Williams. "Were there any visitors at school this afternoon?" he asked.

Mrs. Williams picked up the sign-in sheet and glanced at it. "One parent came to take a sick child home. The regular volunteer who listens to the first-graders read was here, and we had a delivery for the library."

"Nothing unusual," Mr. Quinn said.

"Nothing unusual," Mrs. Williams agreed.

Matt's cheeks started to itch. He rubbed them, one hand on each side of his face. The more he rubbed, the more his cheeks itched. They felt hot, like two glowing coals. His chest itched, too, and he stuck one hand up his T-shirt to scratch.

"I think you were wrong about the candy bar," he said.

"What do you mean?"

"I've got hives."

Denny looked at the boy. His face was puffy, especially around his eyes.

"I itch all over," Matt said. "I need to take one of my pills."

"What pills?"

"The green ones that I take every morning."

"Vitamin pills?"

"No. I take a vitamin pill, too, but now I need the kind I get from the doctor, for my allergies."

Matt kneaded his ears. Denny frowned, watching him. Pink blotches bloomed on the boy's face and neck. Whoever heard of a kid being allergic to chocolate? Still, Matt did look as if he had scrubbed his face with poison ivy. Small bumps like mosquito bites rose on the blotches. Matt's lips seemed swollen.

"Did you ever get hives before when you weren't home?"

"Once I got them at school when I traded my snack for another kid's cupcake."

"What did your teacher, do?"

"The school nurse gave me an allergy pill. Mom had taken some in to the nurse on my first day, in case I ever needed one."

Denny gripped the steering wheel tighter. Nervous perspiration began to soak his T-shirt. He couldn't take the kid to a doctor. No way. "What happens if you don't get a pill?" he asked.

"The hives last longer and itch more. The pill makes them go away."

"You'll have to itch, then."

"I'll take a pill as soon as we get home. I know where Mom keeps them."

"Forget the pills. We're not going there."

"You said we're going home."

"We are. We're going to my home, which is now our home. You're going to live with me from now on. We'll have a great time, me and you."

Matt shook his head. "I don't want to live with you."

"Too bad."

"I want to call my mom."

"Hey, this was her idea. She said to be a good boy and do what I say."

"What about my clothes and my toys and my blankie?"

"She's going to mail everything to you. The pills, too. Not that you'll need your old clothes or toys. I bought everything new for you—a PlayStation with lots of games, and a DVD player and a bunch of movies and a Game Boy."

Matt stared at the man. "Are you rich?" he asked.

"You better believe it, kid. I hit it big last week, so once you get to my place, you can have anything your little heart desires."

Matt thought about that. Mom wouldn't let him have a PlayStation because she thought most of the games were too violent. He had a few movies but not DVD movies. He wondered if Mom really knew where he was going and about all the computer games.

His father's name was Denny Thurman, but how did Matt know that's who this man was? He'd never seen his dad; he didn't know what his dad looked like. Maybe this man was only pretending to be Denny Thurman. "How do I know you're really my dad?" he asked.

"What? My own kid wants to see identification?" Denny pulled a wallet from his hip pocket, then tossed it to Matt. "All right. If you don't trust me, look at my driver's license."

Matt flipped open the wallet and peered at the driver's license, wishing he could read. The photo was this man's face. The license must say Denny Thurman; if it didn't, the man wouldn't show it to him.

Denny scowled while the kid examined his driver's license. This was not going the way he had planned. Not at all. Tim and Thomas never got red spots on their faces. They didn't question everything Winston said.

Matt closed the wallet and handed it back.

"Satisfied?" Denny asked. "Convinced I'm not lying to you? I'm really your dad?"

Matt nodded, but he didn't know what to think. This man really was his father, yet he knew not everything the man said was true. Mom would never have sent Matt to live somewhere else without talking to him about it first, and she certainly wouldn't have let him go without his clothes or his allergy pills.

Something didn't add up. First the man said Pookie was hurt when Pookie wasn't, and now he wasn't going to take Matt home. A terrible suspicion formed in Matt's mind. Had he made a horrible mistake when he got in this car?

Matt rubbed his face some more. He didn't like this man, even if he was his dad. "What about Bonnie?" he asked. "Is she going to live with us?"

"She isn't my kid. You are."

"Bonnie will be mad when she finds out Pookie came with me."

"We don't care what Bonnie thinks. Forget about her."

"I don't want to forget Bonnie. I want to go home."

"Be quiet," Denny said. "You're giving me a headache."

The uncertainty flowing through Matt's mind jelled into conviction. He should never have gotten into the car with this man, whether Pookie was there or not.

"I'm going to sit in back with Pookie," Matt said. He unbuckled his seat belt and started to climb over the seat. He stopped, looking down at the floor. "Pookie's gone!" he cried. "He isn't here!"

Denny shrugged.

"He must have jumped out when we stopped at the bathroom," Matt said, "and we didn't see him go. We have to turn around!"

"Forget it."

"*Forget it?* We can't drive off and leave him behind."

"Sure we can."

"Pookie's old," Matt said. "He can hardly see."

"Calm down. He's fine."

"He isn't fine! He's loose at the park. We have to go back and get him. He'll get hit by a car!"

"He won't get hit. I tied him to a post."

Matt glared at Denny. "You left him at Marymoor Park on purpose?"

"Stupid dog stunk up the whole car."

"That wasn't his fault. You're the one who said to feed him chocolate." He put his hand on Denny's arm. "You have to turn around! We can't leave Pookie by himself!"

"Let's get something straight here," Denny said as he pushed Matt's hand away. "I call the shots. I make the decisions, not you, and the sooner you learn that, the better off you'll be."

"Pookie will be scared. He won't know where he is."

"The dog's lucky I left him at the park. I could have got rid of him."

Matt's voice was only a whisper. "What do you mean?"

Denny pulled his T-shirt up, revealing the gun.

Matt stared. He'd never seen a real gun before.

"Zip your lip about the dog, understand? The mutt was nothing but trouble."

Matt shrank into the seat, leaning against the door, as far from Denny as possible.

They rode in silence for a minute.

"I bought a bunch of board games," Denny said. "Stuff like Monopoly. I used to play Monopoly when I was a kid."

"You said I could have anything I want at your house," Matt said.

"That's right. You got it made, kid."

"I want Pookie."

Denny gave Matt a disgusted look. "Correction: You can have anything you want except a dog."

Two tears trickled down Matt's cheeks, making shiny trails across the red blotches.

"What are you sniffling about? Any normal kid would be thrilled to get every new toy and game."

"Why did you bring Pookie if you don't like him?"

Denny didn't reply.

Let the kid figure it out for himself.

CHAPTER 7

Bonnie ran out of the school office when she saw her mom's car. Mrs. Sholter stopped in the bus zone, jumped out, then put an arm around her daughter's shoulders as they hurried inside.

"He didn't come to the bus," Bonnie said, "so I went to his room and he wasn't there. We've looked everywhere."

Mrs. Jules explained about the hall pass and how she'd checked in the boys' bathroom. Mr. Quinn told about calling the bus drivers and Matt's friends. Other teachers said they had searched the classrooms and the playground.

"We need to call the police," Mrs. Sholter said. She

took a phone from her purse and dialed 911. Everyone in the office listened to the call.

"The police are coming," she said when she hung up.

Teachers wove in and out of the office, asking if Matt had been found yet. Several walked back through every room in the school again, checking closets, restrooms, and the cafeteria for any sign of the missing boy. By the time the police arrived, the staff felt positive Matt was not on the school grounds.

The policeman, Officer Calvin, asked the same questions Mr. Quinn had asked, plus a few more.

"Would he have left the school grounds by himself? To buy candy, perhaps?"

"Absolutely not," Mrs. Sholter said.

"Would he have left with someone else—maybe accepted a ride home?"

"No," Mrs. Sholter said.

"He always rides the bus with me," Bonnie said.

"Did anyone other than staff come to the school this afternoon?"

Mrs. Williams said, "A parent picked up a sick child, a volunteer came to hear the first-graders read, and a package was delivered to the library."

"I didn't get any package today," Mrs. Payton said.

Everyone turned to look at the librarian.

Mrs. Williams picked up the sign-in sheet. "A delivery man came at two twenty-five, with a box for the library. He signed in and took a visitor's badge, and I told him how to find the library." She frowned. "He didn't sign out, though. I didn't notice before; he never signed out." She counted the badges in a small box next to the sign-in sheet. "He didn't return the badge, either."

"I never got a delivery," Mrs. Payton repeated.

Officer Calvin asked, "What company was the deliveryman with?"

"UPS," Mrs. Williams said. "He said he had a package for the library and—"

"Are you sure he said UPS?" Officer Calvin asked. "Was it the regular driver?"

Mrs. Williams ran one hand nervously through her hair. "I didn't recognize him, but he said he was from UPS. He carried a box and a clipboard, and he had on a brown UPS uniform."

"Did you see his truck?" the officer asked.

"I didn't look for his truck."

"Would someone call UPS, please?" Officer Calvin said.

Mr. Quinn looked up the UPS number and called. It took a while to get a live person on the line, but when he did, he explained what had happened. He gave the school's address. Then he put one hand over the telephone mouthpiece and whispered, "She's checking."

A moment later he said, "Are you certain?" Then, after a pause, he said, "Thank you. Yes, I'll let you know."

Even before Mr. Quinn hung up, Bonnie knew from his expression what he was going to say.

"UPS had no delivery scheduled here today," Mr. Quinn reported.

Mrs. Williams covered her mouth with one hand, her eyes brimming with tears.

"This isn't your fault," Mr. Quinn said. "You had no reason to suspect the man wasn't who he said he was."

"He lied," Mrs. Jules said. "Maybe he came here to try to steal a child and he saw Matt alone."

Bonnie's throat felt tight, the way it always did when she came down with a bad cold.

Officer Calvin said, "It appears Matt was by himself at the wrong time."

Mr. Quinn pounded his fist on the countertop. "We tried to have good security," he said. "We tried to prevent something like this. We even had an assembly on what to do and say if approached by a stranger."

"It's hard to prevent every possibility," the officer said.

"Matt *knows* not to go anywhere with a stranger," Mrs. Sholter said. "We talked about it many times. He's been told to scream and run away if anyone tries to take him."

"None of the staff noticed anything unusual," Mr. Quinn said. "Nobody heard Matt yell."

"He would never leave with someone he doesn't know," Bonnie insisted.

The police officer shook his head. "Even kids who know better sometimes get tricked," he said. "The man probably lied to him, and Matt believed what he was told."

"Are you saying you think Matt went willingly?" Mrs. Sholter asked.

"It happens, even with kids who've been taught all the right things. The trouble is, we can't figure out in advance what some crook might say."

"I can't believe Matt would do that."

Bonnie couldn't believe it, either.

"I'll need a photo of Matt as soon as possible," Officer Calvin said, "and a full description, including the clothes he wore today. I believe this case warrants issuing an Amber Alert."

"What's that?" asked Bonnie.

"Matt's description will be broadcast immediately on the emergency alert network. It's the system used for severe weather emergencies such as tornadoes or a volcanic eruption. An Amber Alert will get Matt's description out to the public instantly with messages on the highway reader boards and on radio and TV. Thousands of people will be looking for him within an hour."

"Thank you," Mrs. Sholter said.

"I wish we could broadcast a description of the abductor or the vehicle Matt left in. More than once a motorist has spotted a car that police were looking for and called to report its location. But a good description of the boy might be enough."

Mrs. Sholter opened her wallet, took out a picture of Matt, and handed it to Officer Calvin.

"When was this taken?" he asked.

"Two weeks ago."

"Good. You wouldn't believe how many parents don't have a recent picture of their kids. One woman gave me a snapshot taken at her daughter's third birthday party; the girl was ten years old when she disappeared."

Bonnie said, "Mom's always taking pictures of us, for our scrapbooks and to send to our grandparents."

"We'll put Matt's picture on the TV news and give it to the papers. Pictures work. People see a photo of a cute kid like this, and they pay attention. They look for him."

"I always thought the police waited twenty-four hours to declare a person missing," Mr. Quinn said.

"An adult, yes. Adults often leave home voluntarily without telling anyone. In a case like this, with a child, the faster we move, the better. We don't use the Amber Alert often, but I think it's justified today."

"What can we do to help?" Bonnie asked.

"First tell me what Matt was wearing."

Mrs. Sholter said, "Jeans, a blue Mariners T-shirt, and white shoes—the kind with heels that light up when you walk."

"As soon as I call this in, I'd like to bring a police dog to your home and let him sniff Matt's clothes—maybe the pajamas he slept in last night."

"Of course," Mrs. Sholter said. She gave the address.

Bonnie could tell Mom was struggling to keep her emotions under control. Her voice sounded tight, and she kept fingering the strap on her shoulder bag.

"Do you want to ride with me?" the officer asked. "Or would you like me to follow you?"

"I'll drive; you can follow me," Mrs. Sholter said. "I'll need to have my car."

"Is there anything more any of us can do?" Mr. Quinn asked.

"Please stay here," the officer said. "Another officer will be here shortly, to question everyone and to get a description of the man who claimed to be with UPS."

Mrs. Williams said, "I know exactly what he looked like. He had curly black hair and a mustache and there was a tattoo of a flower on one arm—a rose, I think. I'd recognize him, or his picture."

"Why would anyone take Matt?" Bonnie asked.

"Because he happened to be there," Officer Calvin said. "A crime of opportunity."

Bonnie and her mother rode home without talking. The police car followed. Usually Mrs. Sholter parked in the garage, but this time she pulled up in front of the house. Officer Calvin parked behind her. She opened the front door and motioned for the police officer to come inside as a second squad car parked behind the first one.

"The Amber Alert has gone out," Officer Calvin said. Then he introduced Detective Morrison.

"I have a canine partner," Detective Morrison said. "I'd like to bring him in, and let him smell clothing Matt wore recently."

"You'd better shut Pookie in the kitchen," Mrs. Sholter told Bonnie. "He's still asleep, but he might smell another dog and get in the way."

"Pookie's your dog?" Officer Calvin said.

"Not much of a watchdog, I'm afraid," Mrs. Sholter said.

"He's old," Bonnie explained. "He doesn't see or hear very well, but he's a great dog."

Detective Morrison went out to get her K-9 dog.

Bonnie headed for Pookie's basket in the kitchen. When it was empty, she looked under the dining-room table and in her bedroom. She checked all of Pookie's favorite napping spots, then checked the backyard. She whistled and called.

Bonnie rushed back into the living room. "Mom!" she said. "Pookie's gone!"

CHAPTER 8

"Pookie's gone?" Mrs. Sholter repeated, as if she couldn't possibly have heard correctly.

"I looked in his bed," Bonnie said, "and under the table where he likes to sleep, and then I looked in the backyard. He isn't here."

"Could he have gotten out of the yard accidentally?" Officer Calvin asked. "Is there a gate that might have been left open?"

"There is a gate," Mrs. Sholter said, "but we only use it when we put the trash can in the alley for the trash collector."

"The gate's closed," Bonnie said. "I checked."

"Might someone have let him out on purpose? A neighbor, perhaps? Does Pookie bark a lot?"

Bonnie could follow Officer Calvin's thoughts. "Pookie hardly ever barks anymore," she said. "If someone came in the yard, he probably wouldn't even notice."

"If he did, he'd wag his tail and hope to get petted," Mrs. Sholter said.

Detective Morrison returned with a German shepherd. "This is Spike," she said.

"The family dog is missing," Officer Calvin said.

Bonnie saw the two police officers exchange a glance, the significant kind of look adults give each other when they know something the kids don't know.

Fear had flickered at the edge of Bonnie's mind all morning, but it had been a dull fear, without a name. As she looked at Pookie's empty bed, a sharp, specific fear wrapped around her. Matt was missing, and so was Pookie. What if they never came home? She might never see her brother or her dog again. The tears Bonnie had successfully held back at school now spilled out.

"Do you think Pookie's disappearance is connected to Matt's?" Mrs. Sholter asked the police.

"It might be," Detective Morrison said.

"Let's make sure the dog isn't here," Officer Calvin said.

A thorough search of the house and yard turned up

no Pookie, nor did it yield any sign the house had been broken into.

Bonnie and her mom called Pookie, both in the alley and up and down the sidewalk in the front of the house, in case he had somehow been let out. Pookie did not come.

"Let's have Spike smell those pajamas," Detective Morrison said. "Then I'll take him over to the school."

Bonnie led everyone upstairs to Matt's bedroom. "He keeps his pajamas under his pillow," she said.

"Don't touch them," Detective Morrison cautioned. She lifted the pillow. Matt's pajamas were scrunched into a ball, as usual.

When Mrs. Sholter saw them, she started to cry.

Detective Morrison led Spike toward the bed and pointed.

The dog sniffed the pajamas.

"Matt," said Detective Morrison. "Find Matt." She put Matt's pajamas in a bag and took them with her. She and Spike returned to their car and drove away.

"Does anyone else have a house key?" Officer Calvin asked Mrs. Sholter.

"Bonnie has one."

Bonnie held up the chain she wore around her neck; the key dangled from the chain.

"We also have one hidden outside. We put it there after I accidentally locked myself out."

"Let's see if it's still there," Officer Calvin said. "I hope you don't keep it under the doormat. Thieves look there first."

Bonnie and her mom went out the kitchen door, followed by the police officer. Bonnie counted five fence boards from the corner, then picked up a small rock from the base of the fence. The extra key was taped to the bottom of the rock.

"It's here," she said.

"Who else has a key?" Officer Calvin asked. "Your husband?"

"I'm single."

"Ex-husband?"

Mrs. Sholter leaned against the fence as if her legs were too weak to hold her up. "My first husband, Bonnie's father, was a firefighter who died when a burning roof collapsed on him. I married again two years later, but the marriage was a disaster and I filed for divorce after only three months. Seven months later, Matt was born."

"What is Matt's father's name?"

"Denny Thurman."

"Is this where you lived with him?"

"No. I bought this house two years ago."

"Has there been a recent disagreement about Matt's custody or visitation rights or support payments?"

"Denny has no visiting rights," Mrs. Sholter said, "and I didn't ask him to pay child support. He wouldn't admit the baby was his; as soon as he found out I was pregnant, he vanished, and I haven't heard from him since."

"Then you don't think he might have taken Matt?"

"No. He doesn't like kids; that was one of our problems."

"I didn't like him, either," Bonnie said. "I was glad when he left."

Officer Calvin nodded as if to say *I don't blame you.*

"We all make mistakes," Mrs. Sholter said. "Marrying Denny Thurman was the biggest mistake of my life. The only happy result was Matt."

"We'll check him out. A high number of abducted children are taken by the noncustodial parent."

"Not this time," Mrs. Sholter said. "He doesn't even know if I had a boy or a girl."

"Do you know where he lives?"

"The last I knew, he was living in Reno, but that was six years ago. He always moved often, to get out of paying his gambling debts."

"Would Matt recognize him, maybe from a picture?"

"No."

"Can you think of anyone at all who would want to take Matt? Is there someone Matt would know, someone he'd go with willingly?"

"He'd know lots of people—neighbors or friends or people from church—but he would not leave school with any of them unless I had told him it was okay."

Bonnie said, "If the same person took Pookie, how did they get in? Matt doesn't have a house key, and the one under the rock is still there."

"I think he took Pookie first," Officer Calvin said. "He might have used the dog to get Matt to go with him."

"Then it *wasn't* a crime of opportunity," Mrs. Sholter said. "Matt didn't happen along at the wrong time by accident. If whoever took Matt came here first and got Pookie, then that person set a trap specifically for Matt."

"It's one possibility," Officer Calvin said.

Who would do that? Bonnie wondered. She couldn't think of a single person who would commit such a crime.

"We'll check the house for fingerprints," Officer Calvin said, "and call the animal shelters."

"Pookie is microchipped," Bonnie said. "If he gets scanned, the scanner will show our number."

Officer Calvin called the police station and gave

Pookie's description. "Please call the humane society, PAWS, animal control, and the other shelters," he said. "Have them notify us immediately if anyone brings in such a dog."

Bonnie didn't expect that to happen, though. Dogs brought to shelters by someone other than their owners are usually strays. Pookie had not wandered away accidentally; he had been stolen.

This, Bonnie thought, is worse than any bad dream I ever had.

She hugged herself, trying not to shiver.

CHAPTER 9

Matt stared out the car window, fighting nausea. He always got carsick easily, and now his stomach rumbled from the chocolate he'd eaten. He closed his eyes and breathed slowly.

He knew he should stay alert. He should try to figure out where he was, so when he got a chance to call home, he could tell his mother how to find him.

Matt intended to call as soon as possible. This man couldn't watch him every second. When Denny fell asleep or went to the bathroom, Matt would sneak to the telephone and call Mom.

He knew Denny had driven across the Evergreen Point Floating Bridge, but Matt hadn't recognized anything else. He didn't go to Seattle very often; he knew only major landmarks such as the Space Needle and Safeco Field.

He pressed his forehead against the cool window glass and kept his eyes shut until the car stopped.

They were at the end of a driveway next to a small office building. Denny opened the trunk and lifted out a cardboard box. Matt watched him stomp the box flat, then carry it to a Dumpster at the end of the driveway.

Denny got back in the car and drove off. This time Matt looked out the window, but he still didn't recognize anything. Soon Denny drove into a large apartment complex. The car slowed, going over a series of speed bumps. Rows of buildings, each with adjoining carports, lined the driveway. The road turned several times, but the buildings they passed all looked the same.

The car clock said 4:48. Tears puddled in Matt's eyes. Mom got off work at 4:30; she got home at 4:45.

I should be home now, Matt thought as he rubbed his itchy arms. I should be playing with Pookie or eating an apple. I should be telling Mom about the movie we saw at school today or throwing my ball at the garage.

Sometimes the three of them took Pookie for a walk before dinner or went out together to buy groceries or run errands. Whatever Mom and Bonnie were doing, Matt wished he were doing it with them.

The car stopped in one of the carports. "Hop out," Denny said. "We're home."

Matt followed the man up a flight of stairs and watched as he unlocked an apartment door. Inside, he saw dozens of new computer games and toys. A scooter leaned against the wall next to the door, and stuffed animals covered one end of the couch. A stack of unopened board games towered on an end table. Matt recognized Clue and Candyland. The living room looked like a toy store.

Matt looked around for a telephone but didn't see one.

"Want to watch a movie?" Denny asked.

"No. I want to call my mom." Matt expected Denny to refuse. He had decided Denny was lying; Mom didn't know where Matt was. He figured he'd have to call when Denny didn't know.

"Okay," Denny said.

"I can call her?"

"Sure. She probably wants to talk to you, too, and I need to let her know you got here safely. What's the number? Save me looking it up in my book."

Surprised, Matt gave the phone number. Maybe

Denny hadn't lied. If he had, he'd never let Matt talk to his mom.

Denny took a cell phone out of his pants pocket and punched all the numbers except the last one. Instead of seven, he hit "off." He held the phone to his ear, turning his head so Matt could see his face as he talked.

"Hello," he said. "Is Anita there?"

He paused, as if listening. Then he said, "What? Who is this?" He looked shocked. "What happened?" he asked. "When?"

After a few seconds, he said, "Oh, no!"

Matt pulled on his earlobe. Denny was hearing bad news.

"That's terrible!" Denny said.

"Is that Bonnie?" Matt asked. "I want to talk to her." He reached for the phone, but the man shook his head and motioned for Matt to be quiet.

"This is Denny Thurman," the man said, "Matt's father. I picked up Matt at school today because Anita wanted him to stay with me for a while. I called to let Matt talk to her." He paused again. "Anita planned to send some of Matt's clothes to me, and his allergy pills. Can you mail them?" He gave an address. "Thank you," he said. "Yes, I'll tell Matt."

Denny put the phone back in his pocket, then turned to Matt.

"Your next-door neighbor answered the phone," Denny said.

"Mrs. Watson?"

"Right. Mrs. Watson."

"Why did she answer our phone? Where's Mom?"

"I have some sad news," Denny said. "Your mother and your sister died in a car wreck this afternoon."

Horror crept up the back of Matt's neck. "Mom's dead?" he whispered. "Bonnie, too?"

"Afraid so."

Matt sat down, his mind whirling like the Spinner ride at the county fair. Was Denny telling him the truth, or was this another trick, like when he said Pookie was hurt?

"What happened?" Matt asked.

"A little while ago, they headed for the grocery store," Denny said. "Someone ran a stoplight and hit their car."

Disbelief wedged in Matt's throat like dry cracker crumbs. His voice cracked as he forced out the words, "Did anyone call nine-one-one? Did the ambulance come?"

"An ambulance came and the police came, but they were too late. They did CPR, but your mom and

Bonnie were already gone. Dead at the scene. The other driver died, too."

Matt felt as if he'd been punched in the stomach and had the wind knocked out of him. Head bent, he hugged himself and rocked gently. I'll never see Mom again, he thought. Or Bonnie. Mom will never again tuck me in at night or call me to get up in the morning. He took quick, shallow breaths, trying to wrap his mind around the unbelievable.

I'm a genius, Denny thought. What a flat-out brilliant idea! The kid had bought the story hook, line, and sinker. The one problem Denny had worried about—that Matt would call home when Denny wasn't watching—was solved.

Matt said, "Did Mrs. Watson call Grandma and Grandpa?" They'll come to get me, he thought, and take me to Arizona to live with them.

"Mrs. Watson hasn't been able to reach your grandparents."

"They're on a trip."

"Right. Mrs. Watson said she thought they were traveling."

Grandma and Grandpa often traveled in their RV. They liked to visit new places and learn about the local history. Mom had told him they were leaving, but Matt couldn't remember where they were headed this time.

"They have a phone in the RV," Matt said. "I don't know the number, but it's probably in Mom's directory."

"Your neighbor is trying to find it."

It's all true, Matt thought. The accident really happened. Why else would Mrs. Watson be at his house, trying to call Grandma and Grandpa?

"Mrs. Watson says she'll send your things as soon as she can."

Matt nodded, too shocked to care about his clothes or his allergy pills or even his blankie.

"It's a good thing you came with me today," Denny said, "or you'd be dead, too."

Matt shuddered. He wanted to cry, but his tears had dried up into a hard, little ball deep inside his head.

Matt had memorized his phone number long ago. Mom had drilled it into him when he was only three. "If you are ever in trouble," she said, "call home, even if it's the middle of the night." Matt knew how to place a collect call, in case he was out of the local area and had no money.

None of that knowledge would help him now. He had no one to call. Why dial his own number if Mom and Bonnie would never be there again?

With Mom and Bonnie dead, Matt had no choice but to stay with Denny until he could talk to Grandma and Grandpa. Matt was sure they would come for him as soon as Mrs. Watson told them what had happened, but when would that be?

Denny put soap on his hand and scrubbed off the temporary rose tattoo. Whistling cheerfully, he got out bread, mustard, and a jar of pickles. He took the bag of steak from his pocket and sliced it into thin strips. "I'm hungry," he said. "Do you want a sandwich?"

Matt shook his head no.

"I have peanut butter, if you don't want steak."

Matt shook his head again. How could Denny think about food when Mom and Bonnie were dead? Matt had never known anyone who died, but he knew when it happened the person was gone forever and you never saw them again for the rest of your life.

Bonnie once told Matt, "The day my dad died was the worst day of my life. It was the worst day of Mom's life, too."

Matt had nodded, but he hadn't really understood. Now he knew what she meant. This was the worst day of his life.

The phone rang. Matt went closer as Denny answered, hoping it was Grandma.

"Celia!" Denny said. "Glad to hear from you. I'm looking forward to coming over in the morning." After a pause, Denny said, "Oh. Well, sure, next weekend will work. I wouldn't want to come when the boys are sick."

Denny hung up, disappointed. He would have to wait a whole week to introduce Matt to Celia and Winston. For the first time ever, Denny wanted to see his nephews, and now the little brats had stomach flu.

He sighed and slathered steak sauce on his sandwich. The phone rang again. Denny said, "Hello."

"It's Bronco. You owe me five grand."

Hearing the familiar sandpapery voice on the phone made Denny's stomach knot up. How had Bronco gotten his new phone number?

"Hey, no problem, man," Denny said, trying to sound calm. "I've got your money. I would have brought it to you today, but I had some personal business to take care of. I'll bring it tomorrow."

"I need it tonight."

"Well, sure, I can get it to you tonight. It'll take me a while to get there; I've moved."

"I know. I'm parked in front of your new place right now."

Denny swallowed. How had Bronco learned his new address so quickly? He wiped the perspiration from his upper lip. "I'll be right down."

"I'm waiting."

Denny's hand shook as he clicked the phone shut.

He took an ice-cream carton out of the freezer, removed the lid, and pulled out a thick wad of money. He'd won big on the horse races last week—big enough to pay Bronco off with some left over—but he shuddered to think what would have happened tonight if he had not had the cash. He knew a guy who had run out on Bronco once without paying what he owed. The guy's house had burned down, and the cops never caught the arsonist.

As he counted out five thousand dollars, Denny saw Matt's eyes get huge. The boy looked stunned.

He's a cute kid, Denny thought, with those big brown eyes and thick blond hair. Winston and Celia would love him. Denny paused, looking at Matt, and a slow smile curved across his face.

Why hadn't he thought of this at the start? From now on, the boy was his ticket to financial freedom.

After Winston and Celia met Matt, Denny would explain he urgently needed money because he was going to raise his son himself. He'd mention allergy pills and clothes. He'd say the kid needed braces on his teeth.

Denny's grin spread. His money problems were solved! Winston and Celia were suckers for kids, and they had no other nephews or nieces. Once they met Matt, they'd be glad to help out.

His sister and brother-in-law had money up to their eyebrows. Winston had started his own business, something to do with computer software, while he was still in college and had sold it for millions eight years later. Then, instead of leading the easy life, Winston had started another company. It, too, was a success.

"You're a workaholic," Denny had said.

"Better than being a bum," Winston had replied.

Denny put the ice-cream container back in the freezer with steady hands. Thanks to Matt, he'd never have to fear the Broncos of the world again.

Matt watched Denny stuff the money in his jacket pocket. He had never seen so much cash. Denny had told the truth when he said he was rich.

"I'll be right back," Denny said. "Make yourself at home."

Matt sat on a wooden chair and looked at his lap. His head ached. He itched all over. Worst of all he felt a deep sorrow unlike any emotion he'd experienced before.

I don't like Denny Thurman, Matt thought. I always thought if I ever met my dad I'd like him a lot, but I don't like this man. He isn't even sad! Mom and Bonnie got killed, but he's acting as if Mrs. Watson told him Mom and Bonnie were on a vacation.

Matt longed to bury his face in Pookie's fur and cry.

He wondered if Pookie was still tied to the post or if someone had rescued him by now. Poor old Pookie. He must be so afraid.

Matt felt cold inside, as if he'd swallowed a big chunk of snow and all his blood had turned to ice water. He didn't think he would ever feel warm or safe or happy again.

CHAPTER 10

After the police left, Bonnie said, "I'm going to call Nancy and my other friends. They'll let all the kids know to watch for Matt."

"I don't want you using the phone," Mom said. "Matt might call and get a busy signal. I want to keep the cell-phone line open, too. He memorized both numbers; I know he'll call if he can."

"Is it okay if I use Mrs. Watson's phone?"

Mom nodded.

Bonnie ran next door. Mrs. Watson didn't answer the door, so Bonnie continued down the street to the Largents' house. She told Mrs. Largent what had happened.

"Make as many calls as you want," Mrs. Largent

said. She plucked her toddler from his playpen and held him tight, as if she feared he would disappear next.

Bonnie dialed Nancy's number, but Nancy wasn't home. Of course she isn't, Bonnie thought; she went shopping with Sharon.

She left a message: "Hi, it's Bonnie. Matt is missing, and so is Pookie. The police came with a police dog, and they're searching at the school now. Don't call me because Mom wants to keep the phone line open. I'll call you again when I can."

She felt surreal, as if she couldn't possibly be speaking the words she said. She reached two other friends, who both promised to spread the word.

"I'll alert the other neighbors," Mrs. Largent said.

"Thanks." Then, not knowing what else to do, Bonnie returned home.

Twenty minutes later, Nancy and her mother drove up. "What happened?" Mrs. Tagg asked as Bonnie let them in.

Mrs. Sholter quickly explained.

"I thought you went to the mall," Bonnie said.

"Sharon has a bad headache," Nancy said, "so we decided to go shopping tomorrow. We came here as soon as we heard your message."

"What can we do?" Mrs. Tagg asked.

"I don't know," Mrs. Sholter said. "I can barely think."

"Do you need anything?"

"Maybe the police need help looking for him around the school," Bonnie said.

"We'll go there," Mrs. Tagg said. "Come on, Nancy."

"Can I go with them?" Bonnie asked. "I might be able to help."

Mrs. Sholter hesitated. "Right now, I don't want to let you out of my sight," she said.

"I'll go crazy waiting here, doing nothing."

"I'll stay with her," Mrs. Tagg said, "unless you want her here."

"You can go," Mrs. Sholter said to Bonnie, "but please don't be gone too long."

As they drove to the school, Bonnie told of Pookie's disappearance and the visit from Spike. For once Nancy didn't offer an opinion or make a joke.

Four police cars lined the school driveway. Mr. Quinn, some teachers, and several other people stood near the flagpole, listening to a police officer. As the girls and Nancy's mother joined the group, they heard the officer give directions for searching the neighborhood.

Before he had finished, Detective Morrison and Spike came around the corner of the building. Bonnie hurried over to them, followed by Nancy and Mrs. Tagg.

"Did Spike pick up Matt's scent?" Bonnie asked.

"Yes. He finds it near the side door, then cuts across the playground to the street." She pointed. "Spike stops at the curb and can't find the scent again. We've repeated the search three times with the same results. Matt apparently left the school via that door, then got in a vehicle that was parked on the street."

Nancy took Bonnie's hand.

Bonnie clung to her friend, glad for Nancy's presence. "What happens now?" she asked. "The teachers and others are planning to search this area, but there's no use looking for Matt around here if he was driven somewhere else."

"We still want a door-to-door search of this neighborhood. Someone might have noticed a vehicle parked here. Someone might have glanced out a window and seen Matt and the person he was with as they walked across the playground, or maybe someone walked past as they drove away. We might get lucky and get a description of the vehicle or the abductor or both."

At the word *abductor,* Bonnie's blood ran cold. What a horrible word, she thought. An ugly name for a terrible person.

"The searchers are starting out," Mrs. Tagg said. "Do you still want to join them, Bonnie, or do you want me to drive you home?"

"Join them," Bonnie said. "I'll do anything I can to help find Matt."

CHAPTER 11

"Let's stop at Marymoor Park," Fred Faulkner suggested. "We can walk the path and stretch a bit."

His wife, Ruth, shifted in her seat. "Good idea," she said. "My arthritis is bothering me."

"We used to drive half a day without stopping," Fred said. "Now these old joints stiffen up if I don't get out every hour."

"At least we still go on outings," Ruth said. "Not like some of our friends, who sit at home day after day and get bored with themselves."

"Life's too short to waste any of it," Fred said. "We've been having good times for more than seventy years. No point in getting bored now."

Ruth smiled, and patted his knee. "I did enjoy seeing the Mount Vernon tulip fields," she said.

"Acres of color—and no charge to look at such beauty."

"Maybe there'll be some children on the play equipment," Ruth said. She enjoyed watching the little ones climb and run; it reminded her of when her own girls were small.

Fred pulled into Marymoor Park and stopped the car. After putting a dollar in the parking-fee box, he and Ruth both stretched and headed toward the restrooms.

When Ruth came out, Fred was waiting for her. "Come and see what I found," he said.

Ruth followed her husband to a sign at the side of the restrooms.

"Oh, look at you!" Ruth approached the terrier who was tied to the signpost. "Aren't you a sweet thing?" She let the dog sniff her fist before she petted it. The dog wagged his tail and licked Ruth's fingers.

Ruth looked around. No children climbed the slide; no parents pushed the swings. "Who does he belong to? Is there someone in the men's room?"

"There's nobody else here," Fred said. "We're the only car in the lot."

"Someone drove off and *forgot* their dog?" Ruth said. "How could they?"

"Maybe somebody was walking him, and the dog got tired, so they left him here while they finish their walk."

"I'd be afraid someone would take him."

"Maybe the owner wanted to get rid of him. Maybe he's been abandoned."

"No! Oh, who would do such a thing?" She patted the dog's head. "He isn't wearing a collar," she said. "No license. No ID tag."

"No way to contact the owner," Fred said.

"I can't believe anyone would purposely leave a darling dog like this," Ruth said. "Let's stay here with him for a while, until they come back."

"He looks like an old-timer," Fred said. "He'd probably like to walk around a bit, the same as we did. No telling how long he's been sitting here." He untied the leash from the post, and the dog walked along the path beside him. The tail never stopped wagging.

"We still have half a sandwich left from our lunch," Ruth said. "I'll get it." She took a wicker basket out of the trunk, opened it, and unwrapped half a peanut-butter sandwich.

When Fred returned from walking the dog, Ruth put a piece of sandwich on her palm and held it out. "Here you go," she said. "Here's a treat for you."

"Thanks," Fred said as he reached for the sandwich.

"Not you. The dog."

The dog took it eagerly, smacking his jaws as the peanut butter stuck to the roof of his mouth.

Ruth broke the rest of the sandwich in pieces and the dog gobbled all of them. He nudged her hand, hoping for more.

"He's starving," Ruth said. "He probably hasn't eaten for days."

"He isn't starving," Fred said as he ran his hands down the dog's sides, digging his fingers through the thick fur. "I can't feel his ribs. He's clean and he's been brushed recently and his nails are trimmed. He's been neutered, too. Someone has taken good care of this dog."

"Not good enough."

"Now, Ruthie, you mustn't jump to conclusions. His people will probably drive up any minute with an explanation."

"I wonder what his name is," Ruth said.

A car drove in.

"Here they come now," Fred said.

A couple and two young boys got out and headed for the playground. The boys raced ahead of their parents; none of them paid any attention to Ruth and Fred or to the dog.

"Must not be their dog," Fred said.

Ruth heard music and looked down the path. Three teenage boys with a boom box glided past on Rollerblades. They glanced at the dog but didn't stop.

A van arrived next, followed by a car pulling a trailer loaded with bicycles. The couple in the van got out to walk; the others rode off on their bikes. None of them showed any interest in the dog.

Forty-five minutes and many passersby later, Ruth said, "We've waited long enough. If this dog was left here accidentally, he would have been missed by now."

"We can't leave him here," Fred said. "Look how cloudy his eyes are. I don't think he can see much."

Ruth smiled. "It looks like we have a new friend," she said as she opened the back door of the car.

The dog put his front paws on the seat and tried to jump in, but didn't make it. "He needs a boost," Ruth said.

Fred gave the dog's backside a shove, and the dog scrambled into the car.

"An old arthritic dog will fit right in with us," Ruth said. "I need a boost myself now and then."

"We should leave a note on the signpost," Fred said, "in case someone comes looking for him."

"Hmmph!" Ruth said. "Anyone who would go off and leave a wonderful dog like this tied to a post doesn't deserve to get him back."

"Now, Ruthie. The dog might belong to a family, and one of the kids tied the dog there and the parents won't know he isn't with them until they get home. They could be frantic, worrying about what happened to him."

"Oh, all right," Ruth said. She rummaged in her purse for some paper and fished out a grocery receipt. She wrote on the back: FOUND: DOG—Call 425-555-3268.

"Shouldn't we say he's black and white?" Fred asked. "An older terrier with cloudy eyes?"

"Absolutely not. If someone calls, they'll have to describe him. I'm not giving this dog to just anybody."

Fred took the receipt to the signpost where he'd found the dog, but there was no way to attach it. He went back to the car. "Do you have any tape?" he asked.

"No."

"What about a pin?"

Ruth dug in her purse some more and finally came up with a small sewing kit with a needle in it. Fred put the needle through the receipt and then jabbed it into the wooden signpost.

"Such flimsy paper won't last ten minutes if there's rain or wind," he said as he got back in the car, "but it's the best we can do."

"I've decided to name him Monty," Ruth said. "We'll need to stop on the way home to buy a collar and some dog food. I think we still have Max's ball."

"It's been a while since we had a dog to walk," Fred said. "Remember how Max always woke us up early?"

"It'll be good for us to have a dog again. We'll go out for walks every day whether we feel like it or not. Monty will keep us limber. The best arthritis medicine in the world is a dog."

Fred smiled at his wife. "Rescuing a dog sure beats sitting around getting bored with ourselves," he said.

"You bet it does."

It was nearly six-thirty by the time they arrived home with their purchases. Ruth folded an old blue blanket for a dog bed. Fred filled a cereal bowl with dog food and another with water. Monty slurped the water enthusiastically, spilling some on the floor.

"Do you want to sit and watch the local news?" Fred asked as Monty sniffed all around the house.

"No," Ruth said. "I'm going to heat up some soup for us, and then I want to walk Monty around the outside of our house before it gets dark. If he ever got out by mistake, I want to be sure he knows which house is his."

"I'll walk with you," Fred said. "There's never any

good news anyway. It's always murder and arson and missing children."

"Then why do you watch?"

"Maybe I won't anymore. Maybe I'll walk Monty before dinner every night."

"The good news today," Ruth said, "is that we got a dog!"

CHAPTER 12

The search teams came up empty. No one living around the school had seen Matt or the person who took him. No one had noticed a vehicle parked at the curb where Spike kept stopping.

After an hour of knocking on doors, Mrs. Tagg said, "I think I should drive you home, Bonnie. Your mother will worry if we stay longer."

Bonnie didn't want to quit, but she knew Nancy's mom was right.

When they got to Bonnie's street, Mrs. Tagg couldn't find a place to park. Television crews clogged the front yard; a news helicopter circled overhead. A spokesman from the police department was trying to create order out of the chaos.

"You can drive up the alley," Bonnie said, "and drop me off by our back gate."

"I had planned to come in," Mrs. Tagg said, "but it's clear your mother doesn't need any more visitors."

Bonnie and her mom, along with Officer Calvin, were interviewed by reporters from two newspapers and three television stations. Bonnie found it hard to talk about Matt and Pookie without crying. It was especially difficult when a reporter asked, "Do you think your brother ran away?"

"No!" Bonnie said.

"Maybe he ran off and took the dog with him," the reporter said. "The largest percentage of missing kids are runaways."

Bonnie wanted to scream, "He didn't run away! Quit saying that!" But she knew media help was important, so she tried hard to be pleasant. "He had no reason to run away," Bonnie said. "Matt was happy at home."

"Matt was abducted from his school," Mrs. Sholter said. "Less than fifteen minutes elapsed between when his teacher saw him and when Bonnie reported him missing."

"A police dog picked up Matt's scent in the door-way of the school," Officer Calvin said, "and followed it across the playground to the street. It stopped there, indicating Matt got in a vehicle at that point."

This silenced the reporter with the runaway theory, but it gave Bonnie chills to think of Matt crossing the playground and climbing into a car. She found it hard to believe he would have done such a thing after Mom had warned both of them repeatedly not to ever go anywhere with someone they didn't know. Yet that must be what he had done.

When all the reporters and photographers finally left, Bonnie felt as if she'd run a twenty-mile marathon. The phone rang often as the word spread among their friends. Each time, she answered quickly, hoping it might be Matt.

At eleven p.m. Bonnie and her mom sat together and watched themselves on the Channel Seven news.

Mr. Quinn and Mrs. Jules appeared briefly on the newscast. They said Matt was a good student; everyone liked him. Matt's friend Stanley, looking scared, told how he and Matt had played on the monkey bars during recess.

The screen showed a highway reader board on Interstate 90, with Matt's description in bright lights. The announcer explained the Amber Alert and urged viewers to call 911 if they thought they saw Matt.

The story moved to Jefferson School, where nearly a hundred volunteers still searched the neighborhood for any clues. One man, who said he didn't know Matt, explained why he was there.

"I have a little boy myself," he said, "and I know how I'd feel if somebody took him. I'm here because I want to help."

Then the camera focused on Bonnie and her mom.

Bonnie felt as if she were viewing a movie, watching an actress who looked like her. The look-alike girl talked about her brother and her missing dog. She held up a picture of Pookie while her mom held one of Matt. Mrs. Sholter begged whoever had taken her son to return him unharmed.

"Please bring my dog home, too," the TV Bonnie said, her voice ending in a high squeak as she fought back tears.

The camera zoomed in on the picture of Matt.

"Anyone with information about the missing boy or his dog is urged to call nine-one-one or local police." A number flashed on the screen, followed by a commercial.

After her mom turned off the TV, Bonnie felt numb. She wanted this nightmare to be over.

The police had set up a special telephone system so any calls coming in to the Sholters' number would be monitored by the police. "You may get a ransom demand," Detective Morrison said.

"Ransom!" Mrs. Sholter waved her hand around the modest living room with its worn furniture. "Why would anyone think I can afford to pay a ransom?"

"People who abduct children aren't the great brains of the world," Detective Morrison said. "Clear thinking is not required in order to commit a crime."

The night dragged on. A police car remained parked in the Sholters' driveway. Using their computer, Bonnie and her mom made posters with Matt's picture on them. MATT IS MISSING the posters said.

Mrs. Jules had called earlier to say all the teachers would go out at daylight the next morning to hang posters around town.

"Don't use your own phone number," Detective Morrison had said. "Use the police number, so you don't get any calls from wackos."

"Wackos?" Bonnie said.

"People who call, even though they haven't seen the missing child."

"If they haven't seen him, why would they call?" Bonnie asked. "What would they say?"

"Oh, happy things like 'If you watched your child properly this wouldn't have happened.' One woman used to call every time a child disappeared and claim she'd seen the child's body floating in Lake Washington."

"Gross!"

"People can be cruel. Use my number. Better yet, use the toll-free hotline for the National Center for Missing and Exploited Children. Someone's there to answer the phone twenty-four/seven so you'll be sure not to miss an important call. They know exactly what questions to ask." She had written the number and handed it to Bonnie.

"Are you sure the center knows about Matt?"

"We gave them all the information this afternoon. His picture's already on their Web site. We've also asked for help from the Washington State Patrol's Missing and Exploited Children's Task Force."

Bonnie added information about Pookie to each poster. Knowing other people were trying to find Matt made his return seem possible.

At midnight, Bonnie's mom insisted she lie down for a while. Bonnie knew it was pointless to go to bed; she'd never fall asleep, but she lay on top of her bed in the dark, listening for the phone as tears trickled into her ears.

At six the next morning, Mrs. Jules and Mrs. Payton came to get the posters. "Every teacher at Matt's school and yours, Bonnie, will distribute these," Mrs. Jules said. "There are dozens of other volunteers, as well. We'll make more copies as we need them."

It helps, Bonnie thought, to know the teachers are giving up their Saturday for this.

"We plan to blanket the entire Puget Sound area with posters," Mrs. Payton said.

Mrs. Jules left her cell-phone number. "Call as soon as he's found," she said.

At seven, someone else knocked on the door. Hope surging, Bonnie ran to open it. Mrs. Watson stood on the step holding a pan of warm cinnamon rolls.

Mrs. Watson's curls had a bluish tinge and she always smelled faintly of lilacs. Three years ago when Mrs. Watson turned eighty, she announced she would count backward on future birthdays. Now if anyone asked her age, she said, "Seventy-seven."

"I thought you might need some breakfast," Mrs. Watson said.

"Come in, Mrs. Watson," Bonnie said.

"Is there any word about Matt?"

"No."

Bonnie had eaten nothing the night before; the fragrant rolls smelled delicious. Although cinnamon rolls were her favorite treat, especially Mrs. Watson's homemade cinnamon rolls, she felt guilty for wanting one. How could she think about food when her brother and her dog were missing?

"You have to eat," Mrs. Watson said, "to keep up

your own strength. You won't be any help to the police otherwise."

Mrs. Sholter poured two cups of coffee and invited Mrs. Watson to stay. Bonnie got herself a glass of orange juice to go with her roll. The prism in the window sent rainbows dancing across the tile floor. Maybe that's a good omen, Bonnie thought. Rainbows are a sign of hope. On the other hand, she'd seen rainbows yesterday morning, too, and look what had happened.

"I saw on the news that Pookie's gone, too," Mrs. Watson said.

"The police think someone might have taken Pookie first and then used him to entice Matt to go with them."

"That gives me the all-over shivers," Mrs. Watson said. "It means the person who took Matt came here, too."

Bonnie knew Mrs. Watson was upset in part because she lived so close.

"I wish I'd stayed home yesterday, instead of going to my book club," Mrs. Watson said. "I might have seen or heard something. Maybe Pookie barked."

After Bonnie finished eating, she said, "I'm going to look around outside some more."

Every inch of the yard had been examined the day

before, but she was too antsy to sit still. As she crossed the yard, she looked at the polka-dot garage door. I'd give anything, she thought, to hear a tennis ball hitting the door again.

She went out the back gate then walked up the alley to the corner. When she returned, she spied something red deep in the weeds next to the fence.

When she pushed the tall weeds back, she saw Pookie's collar. She reached for it, then withdrew her hand. The police might find fingerprints on the collar.

Bonnie raced inside. "I found Pookie's collar!" she said. "It's in the weeds out in the alley."

Mrs. Sholter quickly called Officer Calvin. "Don't pick it up," he said. "I'll be right there."

Bonnie returned to the alley. She wanted to be sure nobody else found the collar and took it. Officer Calvin arrived soon and, wearing gloves, carefully picked up the collar and dropped it in an evidence bag.

"So whoever took Pookie went out the back gate," Bonnie said. "They must have parked in the alley and thrown his collar away so he couldn't be identified by our phone number."

"That's as good a theory as any," Officer Calvin said.

"Pookie was probably out in the yard," Mrs. Sholter said, "which explains why nobody broke into the house. Pookie used his doggie door, then the man opened the gate and took Pookie."

Bonnie imagined the scene. Dear old Pookie, plodding outside to do his business, then falling asleep in the sunshine. When the man entered the yard, Pookie probably licked his hand.

"Of course we don't know it was a man," Officer Calvin said. "A woman might have taken Pookie."

Bonnie wondered if a woman might have taken Matt. She knew sometimes women who can't have a baby freak out and steal someone else's baby, but she didn't think they stole six-year-old boys.

Officer Calvin had brought a computer-generated image of the man who had come to the school, pretending to work for UPS. "The secretary gave a detailed description," he said, "especially of his hair, mustache, and tattoo."

Bonnie stared at the drawing, examining the man's eyes and his curly dark hair. She had never felt hatred toward anyone, but as she looked at the drawing she felt such intense dislike for the man that her feelings shocked her.

Mrs. Sholter glanced at the drawing, then covered her face with her hands and turned away, as if she couldn't bear to look.

"Do either of you recognize him?" Officer Calvin asked.

"No." Bonnie and her mom spoke at the same time.

"This image went out last night via e-mail and broadcast faxing," Officer Calvin said. "It's now in the hands of law-enforcement agencies all across the country. The school secretary says it's a good likeness, and the rose tattoo is an excellent clue because it's specific. People notice such things and remember them. Of course we don't know for certain the UPS impostor took Matt."

Officer Calvin doubts everything, Bonnie thought, even the obvious facts. She supposed it was good the police considered all possibilities, but only one scenario made sense: a man dressed as a UPS delivery man stole Pookie, drove to the school, and talked Matt into going somewhere with him. Who had done it? Why? Where were Pookie and Matt now?

Bonnie looked at the drawing again, barely resisting the urge to rip it into pieces.

Since the police were now monitoring the Sholters' phone, Bonnie and her mom left the house together and spent the day distributing more MATT IS MISSING posters. They checked in with Officer Calvin frequently, but there was never any news.

By the time they returned home, Bonnie was worn out. She ate, took a shower, and went straight to bed.

Two hours later, she woke trembling and drenched with sweat. She had dreamed of running alone through tall grass, calling for help.

No, Bonnie thought. I can't start having nightmares again. Matt isn't gone forever, and I'm not alone. Dozens of people are helping us, people we don't even know.

Bonnie longed to have Pookie on her bed again, pawing at the blanket and making little whimper sounds in his sleep.

As her heart rate returned to normal, she remembered reading Nancy's note and wishing she could go to the mall instead of watching Matt. Had Matt been lured away from school at that exact moment? Had he climbed into a car as Bonnie wished she didn't have to take care of him?

CHAPTER 13

On Sunday, the Sholters' house seemed full of what wasn't there. Everywhere Bonnie looked she expected to see Matt or Pookie. She put fresh water in the dog dish, as she did every morning. She set three cereal bowls on the table for breakfast, then put Matt's bowl back in the cupboard.

Even the sun glinting off the prism didn't seem cheerful. Bonnie reached for the milk carton without glancing at the rainbows on the floor.

That afternoon Bonnie made smaller MISSING flyers on the computer. She put Matt's picture on them plus his name and age. She added: *Favorite food: macaroni and cheese. Loves to play baseball.* She put a description of Pookie, too, and said he was also missing.

She used the phone number Detective Morrison had given her.

Bonnie printed the flyers, getting four per sheet of paper. She used red paper because red was Matt's favorite color, but his picture didn't show clearly, so she switched to white paper. She didn't need to please Matt; she needed to find him.

"Pictures work," Officer Calvin had said.

She printed fifty sheets, or two hundred flyers. Nancy helped her cut them.

"I'll give some to everyone at school tomorrow," Nancy said. "I'm sure they already know about Matt, but they can pass the flyers on to people who might not know."

"Thanks," Bonnie said. "Mom said I can take them to the grocery store and hand them out to people shopping."

"What about other towns?" Nancy said. "Whoever took Matt might have gone away from here. I could mail some to my Aunt Judy and Uncle Frank in Richland. I know they'd give out the flyers."

"Good idea. The police are using a national organization for missing kids, but we need to reach people who don't know about that group."

Nancy took a stack of flyers. "I have to go home now," she said. "It's my grandma's birthday, and we're having a party for her. We don't feel like having a party—we'd rather help try to find Matt—but we invited Grandma's friends weeks ago. I'll give all of them one of the flyers."

"Thanks."

"Mom says if Matt isn't found today, I can come over and help again tomorrow, as soon as I get home from school."

Bonnie promised to call if there was any word. After Nancy left, Bonnie thought, Nancy's right. The person who took Matt could have gone anywhere. Matt might not be in Washington State now. Matt could be in Florida or New York or anywhere.

The police had alerted the airport, but what if Matt's kidnapper took a short flight before the word got out? Maybe he flew a private plane. Maybe they took a bus or Amtrak. Matt might be in a car right now, speeding across Iowa.

The possibilities were endless. Bonnie looked at the stack of MATT IS MISSING flyers. They seemed like such a small thing to do in the face of a huge problem.

Bonnie took a deep breath. My flyers may be small, she thought, but they're better than doing nothing, and Matt might still be in the Seattle area. His abductor could be holed up somewhere, waiting for the furor to die down.

She filled a bag with flyers, got on her bike, and headed for the grocery store. One of the clerks gave Bonnie permission to stand at the door and distribute the flyers.

"I saw you on the news last night," the clerk said. "I hope they find your brother real soon. Your dog, too."

In between shoppers, Bonnie had time to think. The Internet was the best way to spread information quickly. She decided to write an e-mail about Matt to all the names in Mom's address book. She would ask everyone to watch for him and to send her message to all the people on their e-mail lists. She could include the Web site that had Matt's picture. Hundreds more people all over the country would instantly be looking for Matt.

The idea was too good to wait. Bonnie left her post at the store and went home to send the e-mail right away. As she turned her bike onto her street, she saw a van from one of the TV stations parked in front of her house. Bonnie's mom was talking to reporters again.

Bonnie's pulse raced. Had Matt been found? She pedaled faster. Mom stood on the porch alone.

If Matt had been found, he would be there with her. Was there bad news? The small seed of fear that had lurked all day in the back of Bonnie's mind quickly blossomed into panic.

As soon as she reached her own house, Bonnie dropped the bike at the curb and listened to Mom's words: "If anyone sees Matt, please call the police immediately." It sounded like a rerun of yesterday's news conference.

Bonnie noticed her mom's eyes were puffy and red. She probably cried half the night the same as I did, Bonnie thought. She retrieved her bike, rode it around to the alley, and put it in the garage.

When the media people left, Mrs. Sholter told Bonnie, "My boss called. He's offered a ten-thousand-dollar reward for information leading to Matt's safe return."

"Wow!" Bonnie said.

"Most people are good," Mrs. Sholter said.

She's right, Bonnie thought. There are bad people in the world, people who steal children and dogs, but there are lots more good people. Dozens of people—maybe even hundreds—were walking the streets today, searching for Matt.

Detective Morrison came to the door. "We heard from someone who thinks he saw Pookie."

"Did he see Matt?" Bonnie asked. "Was Matt there?"

"No. He didn't see Matt."

"Was Pookie running loose or was he with someone?" Mrs. Sholter asked.

"He was with an elderly couple."

"An elderly couple? Are you sure it was Pookie?"

"The caller thinks it was Pookie. He saw them late Friday afternoon."

"Where?" Bonnie asked.

"He was Rollerblading with friends at Marymoor Park, and he saw the dog with a man and woman, both about seventy years old, who stood near some restrooms. The caller didn't notice what kind of vehicle they were driving, but the time would be about right."

"Did he talk to them?" Bonnie asked.

"No. At the time he had no reason to pay attention to the couple or the dog. Then he saw Pookie's picture on television and thought the dog he saw Friday afternoon was the same, so he called. Of course, he could be mistaken; the dog he saw might not have been Pookie."

There she goes again, Bonnie thought. The police didn't seem to believe anything until it was proven.

"We have officers at Marymoor Park right now," Detective Morrison said, "looking for anything useful. The young man who called remembered exactly where he saw the dog."

"If it was Pookie," Bonnie said, "why wasn't Matt there, too?"

"Perhaps he was," Mrs. Sholter said. "That's what the police are trying to find out."

Matt might have been in the bathroom, Bonnie thought, where the boy on Rollerblades didn't see him, or he might still have been in the kidnapper's car.

"Marymoor Park isn't very far," Bonnie said. "Why would the person have gone there?"

"If an elderly couple had Pookie," Detective Morrison said, "I'd like to know where they got him."

"I wonder what their connection is to the man who was at the school," Bonnie said.

"Someone has to notice a small boy and a dog who suddenly show up where they didn't live before," Mrs. Sholter said. "Whoever took them might be able to pretend Matt is a visiting relative, but Pookie's not easy to conceal—he has to go outside regularly. Matt and Pookie together will be hard to hide."

"They may not be together," Detective Morrison said. "Matt's abductor might have given the dog to someone."

"Such as the couple in the park," Bonnie said.

"It's also possible Pookie's disappearance and Matt's aren't connected."

"Pookie's picture has been on TV and in the newspaper," Bonnie said. "Who would keep a dog they know was stolen?"

"Not everyone watches the news or reads the papers," Detective Morrison said.

Bonnie sank into a chair. "It keeps getting worse and worse," she said.

"We'll find Matt and Pookie," Mrs. Sholter said. "We have to find them."

Detective Morrison nodded. "It may take a few days."

Bonnie didn't think she could stand it if it went that long with no word.

"The abductor might try to disguise Matt," Detective Morrison said. "His hair could be cut differently or even dyed a different color. He's probably wearing new clothes by now."

"Maybe they'll dye Pookie's hair, too," Bonnie said.

"I doubt anyone would dye the dog's fur," Detective Morrison said, "but they might shave it off."

"Everyone is looking for a shaggy dog," Bonnie said.

"I know."

"Maybe the man kept Matt, but gave Pookie to the old couple," Bonnie said. "Maybe they're his parents or his grandparents."

"You should go into police work," Detective Morrison said. "You think like a cop. More likely, the person who took Pookie dumped him after he served his purpose of luring Matt into the car."

"Whoever found him thinks he was a stray," Bonnie said.

"Do you know anyone who works for UPS?" Detective Morrison asked.

"No," Mrs. Sholter said.

"Did you in the past?"

"No."

"I thought the man at the school wasn't really a UPS deliveryman," Bonnie said.

"He wasn't. I'm trying to find out where he got the uniform. Maybe he used to work for UPS, or a relative works for them. Maybe it wasn't a real uniform. Anyone could buy a brown shirt and embroider UPS on the pocket. If he wore matching brown pants, he'd look authentic."

"There are so many possibilities," Bonnie said. "How can you sort through everything?"

"I can't," Detective Morrison said. "I start with what seems most important, the most likely to provide a solid lead, and follow through on that. Other officers do the same, one idea at a time."

"We appreciate all you're doing," Mrs. Sholter said.

"By the way, the police in Reno say your ex-husband left there four years ago, leaving twelve unpaid traffic tickets but no forwarding address."

Mrs. Sholter made no comment.

Usually Sundays flew past much faster than school-days, but this one dragged on. Every time the mantel clock struck the hour, Bonnie thought, Another hour without Matt. Another hour without Pookie.

Two women who worked with Bonnie's mom brought a casserole and some potato salad. "You have to eat," they said, "and we didn't want you worrying about what to fix."

Not long after they left, Nancy and her parents arrived with a platter of fried chicken and half a cake. "The cake's left over from Grandma's party," Nancy said.

Matt's friend Stanley and his dad brought a big bowl of macaroni and cheese. Stanley still looked scared.

"This is Matt's favorite meal when he's at our house," Stanley's dad said. "We thought you should have some ready to warm up as soon as Matt gets home."

"Thank you," Bonnie said as she took the bowl.

"Will you have Matt call me as soon as he gets home?" Stanley asked.

Mrs. Sholter promised she would. Then she put the macaroni and cheese in the freezer, to save for Matt's homecoming.

Mrs. Largent, pushing her toddler in his stroller, brought over a pan of lasagna. "When I made our dinner," she explained, "I made extra for you."

When everyone had left, Bonnie looked at all the food and said, "This is what people always do when there's been a death in the family—they bring food." She burst into tears.

Mrs. Sholter hugged her daughter. "It's what people do for each other in any time of trouble. I took a salad to Mrs. Watson after she had surgery, remember? And you baked cookies for Nancy when she broke her ankle."

Bonnie wiped her eyes.

"It's kind of our friends to bring food," Mrs. Sholter said. "They want to help, and it's one of the few things they can do."

She got two plates and handed one to Bonnie. "We may as well eat it while it's fresh."

Bonnie put some potato salad and a piece of chicken on the plate. She hadn't realized how hungry she was until she started to eat. Everything tasted wonderful.

As she bit into a piece of cake she said, "I wonder what Matt is eating."

"Even getting kidnapped probably hasn't dulled Matt's sweet tooth," Mrs. Sholter said. "If he were here, he'd be trying to see how much cake he could eat before I made him stop."

Bonnie smiled, a bittersweet smile. She remembered scolding Matt only a week ago, because when she went to the freezer for some strawberry ice cream, it was all gone. Mom didn't buy ice cream often, and Bonnie was furious when she discovered Matt had eaten the whole quart.

"You little pig," she told him. "Other people like ice cream, too, you know."

For a few seconds, Matt looked ashamed and pulled on his earlobe, the way he always did when he was anxious. Then he dropped to all fours and grunted and snuffled like a pig until Bonnie had to laugh and couldn't stay mad at him.

Oh Matt, she thought. I'd gladly let you eat all the ice cream, if only you were home again.

CHAPTER 14

"Are you going to take me to school today?" Matt asked.

"School?" Denny looked blank.

"It's Monday. I go to school on Mondays. I'm supposed to be there by eight-fifteen."

"Not today. You won't be going to school for a while."

"I'm almost done with kindergarten. I have to finish so I can graduate to first grade."

"You don't have to go back. You've already graduated. You'll start first grade in September."

Denny hadn't thought that far ahead—he hadn't thought beyond the weekend visit with Winston and Celia—but he knew he couldn't enroll the kid in school anywhere in the Northwest. He wished he could. It would get the boy out of the apartment every day.

Denny's nerves jangled when Matt sat around with those big, sad eyes watching everything Denny did. The only thing worse was when the kid pretended to throw a baseball. He actually held an imaginary ball, then pretended to throw it as hard as he could. It was weird.

"What am I going to do until September?" Matt asked. "It's boring here. All you do is watch boxing and horse racing on television and talk on your telephone. I don't have anyone to play with. You should have kept Pookie."

"Boxing and racing are not boring, kid. I make big bucks on the boxers and the horses."

Denny's phone rang, ending the discussion.

On Saturday and Sunday, Matt had listened carefully to all Denny's conversations because each time the phone rang, he had hoped it would be his grandparents. Now he didn't bother to eavesdrop because Denny only talked about numbers and money. Sometimes the calls made Denny excited; often they made him angry. Once he threw the phone across the room, then kicked the refrigerator so hard that the grille fell off the bottom.

Matt wished he could see Mrs. Jules and his classmates. He wanted to tell Mrs. Jules how sad he felt about Mom and Bonnie. Mrs. Jules would be sad, too. He wanted to sit in the story circle and finish his project about windmills and play on the monkey bars with Stanley. Even if he had to go to a different school, it would be better than being cooped up in this dumb apartment all the time. He couldn't even practice his pitching. He didn't have a ball.

"You could buy me a ball," he suggested, "and we could play catch."

"Forget it," Denny said.

"I could throw a tennis ball against the back of the carport."

"I said, forget it! You aren't going outside."

Matt remembered all the times after school when Bonnie had caught balls for him. "Zinger!" she would call, which meant Matt should throw as hard as he could. Matt would take aim at Bonnie's mitt, then throw with all his might.

Matt's throat felt tight. Bonnie would never again be the catcher while Matt practiced pitching.

Stanley's dad played catch with Stanley all the time. Why wouldn't Matt's dad play with him?

Matt recalled once last year when he had asked Mom about his father.

"Your dad and I made a mistake when we got married," she had said. "We thought we loved each other, but we didn't. We didn't know each other well enough."

"Why doesn't my dad ever come to see me? Stanley's parents got a divorce, but he stays with his dad lots of times. Is it because my dad doesn't like me?"

"Of course not," Mom had said. "He doesn't even know you. If he did, he'd love you to pieces, the same as I do, and Grandma and Grandpa do, and Bonnie, and Mrs. Jules and everyone else who knows you."

At the time, Matt had believed her, but now he thought she had been wrong. His dad didn't love him to pieces. His dad didn't even like him.

Matt closed his eyes and silently recited the list he'd made of all the fun things he'd done with Bonnie. Remembering good times helped get him through this bad time.

Bonnie stayed home from school on Monday, and her mom stayed home from work. They talked to reporters, trying to say something different to keep the story in print and on the air even though there was nothing to report.

Bonnie spent an hour at the grocery store handing out flyers. A light drizzle dripped from the gray sky, matching Bonnie's gloomy mood. She wished it would either rain hard or clear up. It was as if the clouds had cried all their tears and now could squeeze out only this faint mist.

At noon, the Office of Emergency Management called off the Amber Alert.

"Why?" Bonnie asked.

"The Amber Alert is most helpful when we have a vehicle description," Detective Morrison said. "By now Matt's photo is on TV and in the newspapers; the public is aware of his disappearance, so using the emergency services is no longer necessary."

Detective Morrison had other disappointing news. The search of Marymoor Park had found no evidence that either Matt or Pookie had been there.

"A crew cleaned that restroom on Saturday," she said. "They emptied the trash cans and picked up any litter from the ground before they mowed the grass. It was a long shot there would be anything linked to Matt, but still it seems incredibly bad luck for the cleaning crew to go there that particular day."

Ever since the report that Pookie had been seen at Marymoor Park, Bonnie had hoped Matt had been there, too, and that he would have left a clue. Matt was smart; he knew how to print his name and he knew his numbers.

Bonnie had fantasized that the police would find MATT and a license number scratched in the dirt with a stick or written in soap on the restroom mirror.

As she listened to Detective Morrison, Bonnie's hope was erased by disappointment. Matt might have been too scared to think about leaving a clue. Maybe his abductor hadn't left him alone long enough for Matt to write his name. Perhaps Matt had never been near Marymoor Park. It might have been some other dog who looked like Pookie.

On Tuesday, Bonnie's grandma and grandpa arrived from Arizona. Usually Bonnie loved it when her grandparents came to visit, but this time was different. Grandma cried a lot; Grandpa looked old and tired. Instead of playing gin rummy and working a new jigsaw puzzle together—as they usually did when Grandma and Grandpa visited—Bonnie put up posters, checked all the animal-shelter Web sites for Pookie, and tried to think of new ways to find Matt.

Since Matt had twin beds in his room, Grandma and Grandpa always slept there while Matt used an inflatable mattress on the floor in Bonnie's room. This time the extra mattress stayed rolled up in its bag, making Bonnie's room seem empty.

The days blurred together like scenery viewed from a fast-moving car. Each day, Bonnie and her mom and grandparents traveled farther from home with their stack of posters, hanging them as far south as Centralia and as far north as Bellingham.

Detective Morrison called or came by every day. One day she said, "I heard from a truck driver who says he saw Pookie tied to a post at Marymoor Park last Friday."

"What about the old couple?" Bonnie asked.

"He didn't see them, just the dog. He described the same area we've already searched, so the report doesn't help."

Another day she said, "We traced Denny Thurman to California. He's been married and divorced twice since you left him."

Mrs. Sholter shook her head. "I wish I could have warned those women," she said.

"We talked to his most recent ex-wife. She said Denny had no kids and no job. From the sound of it, he's still a compulsive gambler. He was convicted once for assault and served six months in prison. The court-appointed psychiatrist called him an antisocial personality who doesn't care who he hurts as long as he gets what he wants. His last known address was in Los Angeles, but he isn't there now."

Assault! Prison! The words sent ripples of horror down Bonnie's spine. She had once lived in the same house with Denny Thurman. He was Matt's father!

"When he wins, he rents a nice place," Mrs. Sholter said. "He eats in good restaurants and buys an expensive car. When he loses, the car gets repossessed. He stays in the nice house or apartment without paying rent until he gets evicted, and then he moves on."

"His fingerprints are in the system. Too bad the only prints we got from your house, gate, and Pookie's collar were the two of you. Does he have any family?"

"An older sister, Celia. I never met her, but Denny talked about her a couple of times. They weren't close, and Denny disliked her husband. His first name was Woodson or Weston or something like that, but I don't remember their last name and I don't know where they lived."

Mrs. Sholter watched Detective Morrison write this information down, then added, "I really think you're wasting your time trying to find Denny. He had absolutely no interest in his child."

"People change," Detective Morrison said, "and we don't have a whole lot of other folks to look for in this case."

No suspects, Bonnie thought, and no clues. How would they ever find Matt?

Bonnie and her family watched the local newscasts and read the papers, hoping there would be articles reminding people to look for Matt, but there weren't. Since there were no new developments in the case, it had been replaced by more recent events.

"It's as if nobody cares anymore," Bonnie said. "We're the only ones who talk about Matt."

"They care," Mrs. Sholter said, "but when there's nothing new to say, the story isn't going to get media attention."

On Thursday afternoon Bonnie said, "Tomorrow is one week since we saw Matt. It seems more like a month."

"Or a year," Mrs. Sholter said.

"Maybe the TV station could make a story out of the fact he's been gone a week," Bonnie suggested. "That would get people looking for Matt again."

"Great idea!"

Mrs. Sholter called the reporter who had broadcast the first story about Matt and asked if she would show the pictures of Matt and Pookie again, on the one-week anniversary.

The reporter agreed.

CHAPTER 15

Fred Faulkner pounded the last nail into the fence board. He straightened, rubbing his aching back. The old terrier plodded toward him, tail wagging.

"All done, Monty," Fred said. "No more missing boards. You can go outside whenever you want without being on the leash."

The dog wagged his tail and followed Fred into the house.

"The fence is fixed," Fred said.

"Good," Ruth said. "Now when Monty needs to go out after dark, he'll be safe and we won't have to go with him."

Fred eased into his favorite chair. "I'm worn out,"

he said. "I'm going to sit here awhile, and watch the news."

"Would you like some coffee?"

"Are there any cookies to go with it?"

"Dinner will be ready soon."

"A man gets hungry, working outside. A cookie won't spoil my appetite."

Ruth disappeared into the kitchen, then returned with a mug of coffee and a chocolate-chip cookie.

"Only one?" Fred said.

"I'm fixing spaghetti. You can eat cookies after dinner."

She went back to the kitchen.

The dog sat next to Fred's chair, laid his head on Fred's knee, and stared at the cookie. Yawning, Fred clicked on the TV and pressed MUTE until the commercials ended. He yawned again. Maybe he'd close his eyes and take a little snooze before dinner.

He pointed the remote at the TV to turn it off, and then froze. The screen showed a picture of the dog who sat beside him.

"Ruth!" Fred yelled as he turned the sound back on again.

She came running. "What is it? What's wrong?"

Fred sat upright in his chair, staring at the TV.

"You know how they always have teasers at the start of the news, to try to get you to stay tuned? Well, one of those teasers was a young girl holding a picture of Monty."

"Are you sure it was him?"

"Of course I'm sure. I know my own dog when I see him."

"But why would—"

"Shhh. The news is starting."

They sat through a report about the budget crisis in the state government, and a story about a ten-car accident on Interstate 5. The weatherman said, "Will the cold front continue through the weekend? My forecast, coming up." Next came pictures of an apartment fire in Oregon.

"Come on!" Fred said. "Tell us about Monty!"

As he said it, Monty's picture appeared on the screen again, along with a picture of a small boy. "Stay tuned for an update on the disappearance of six-year-old Matt Sholter and his dog, Pookie," the announcer said. Another commercial came on.

Fred and Ruth looked at each other.

"Pookie?" Fred said.

The dog's tail thumped the floor.

Ruth felt sick to her stomach. The spaghetti sauce no longer smelled good.

The newscast resumed with a report of an increase in car thefts from local park-and-ride lots, followed by a grinning couple who had won the state lottery.

Finally the announcer said, "One week ago today six-year-old Matt Sholter was abducted from his elementary school. That same day, the Sholter family's dog, Pookie, vanished from their yard. Police believe the dog may have been stolen and used as a decoy to get Matt to go with his abductor. There are no suspects in this case and no clues to the whereabouts of Matt and his dog. Anyone with information is asked to call . . ."

Ruth grabbed a pencil and wrote down the number as the camera focused on a woman holding a picture of a boy, and a girl holding a picture of the dog.

"It's Monty, all right," Ruth said. "We found him a week ago today."

"It wasn't his family who left him tied at Marymoor Park. It was whoever stole him out of his yard."

"Oh, that poor woman," Ruth said. "Losing her boy and her dog."

As the news went on to the next item, Fred clicked off the television. He leaned down and scratched behind the dog's ears. "We have to give him back, Ruthie," he said.

"I know." Fighting back tears, she picked up the phone and dialed the number.

Bonnie, her mom, and her grandparents watched the Friday newscast together.

"Someone, somewhere, has to know something," Mrs. Sholter said. "Matt and Pookie can't vanish without a trace."

Twenty minutes after their segment of the newscast ended, the telephone rang. Bonnie answered.

"I had a call from someone who says she and her husband have Pookie," Detective Morrison said. "They saw his picture on the television news a few minutes ago. It was the first they knew about the case. Everything the woman told me fits—her description of Pookie and when they found him. You're about to get your dog back."

Bonnie clutched the telephone as goose bumps slithered down her arms. "What about Matt?"

"She had no information about Matt, only Pookie."

"Where is Pookie now?" Bonnie asked. "Where does this woman live?"

"She and her husband live near Pine Lake. They're bringing him to the station," Detective Morrison said. "I'll come with them to your house."

Bonnie cupped her hand over the mouthpiece and

called to her mother and grandparents in the kitchen. "Somebody found Pookie!" She spoke into the telephone again as the others rushed into the living room. "Where did they find him?" Bonnie asked.

"He was tied to a post at Marymoor Park, the area we've already searched. It seems the skater who called was right; he did see Pookie there with an older couple. These folks are both seventy-four. When nobody came for the dog, they thought Pookie had been abandoned by his family."

"He was abandoned," Bonnie said, "but not by his family."

"The people who found him are Fred and Ruth Faulkner," Detective Morrison said. "We should arrive in about an hour."

Bonnie hung up the phone. "Pookie's safe!" she cried as she hugged her mother. "He's coming home!"

Forty-five minutes later, Detective Morrison parked in front of the Sholter residence, followed by another car. Bonnie, who had been watching out the window, dashed outside.

"Pookie!" she said as she looked through the window into the backseat. "It *is* him," she called back to her mother and grandparents, who had followed her out of the house. "It's really Pookie!"

A gray-haired couple got out. The woman opened

the back door of the car. Pookie scrambled out and pushed his head into Bonnie's arms. She dropped to her knees to hug him. Pookie's tail waved back and forth like a flag at the Fourth of July parade. He made happy little yips as he licked Bonnie's face.

"I guess there isn't any doubt," Ruth said.

Mrs. Sholter introduced herself. "I can't thank you enough for bringing Pookie back to us," she said.

"He's a fine dog and we love him dearly," Ruth said, "but when we saw you people on the TV news, we knew what we had to do."

"Please come inside," Detective Morrison said, "and tell me again exactly where and when you found the dog."

Ruth and Fred told their story, being careful to put in every detail they could remember. While they talked, Bonnie sat on the floor with her arms around Pookie.

When Fred told about using a needle to put the FOUND DOG notice on the signpost, Detective Morrison said, "Either it blew away or the cleanup crew tossed it out, not knowing it might be important."

"Thank you for taking good care of Pookie," Bonnie said.

"We enjoyed having him," Ruth said.

"I've been so scared," Bonnie said. "I thought he was lost and hungry, or he'd been hit by a car."

"May I give you something for your trouble?" Mrs. Sholter asked.

Fred looked insulted. "It was no trouble," he said. "No trouble at all."

"At least let me pay you for the dog food and the new collar and whatever else you bought for him."

The Faulkners refused to take a penny. "Monty—I mean Pookie—gave us a lot of pleasure last week," Fred said. "We'll miss him."

"I wish Pookie could talk," Bonnie said.

"So do I," said Detective Morrison.

"Come along now, Ruthie," Fred said. "We need to get on home."

Ruth's voice quavered as she said good-bye to the dog.

"You may come to visit anytime you want," Mrs. Sholter said. "Pookie would love to see you again, and so would we."

"I hope you find your boy soon," Ruth said.

Detective Morrison walked with the Faulkners to their car. As they got in, she told them, "Many of the local animal shelters have special programs to help senior citizens adopt a dog or cat at little or no charge.

You might want to call the Humane Society or PAWS or Pasado's Safe Haven. There are always good dogs at the shelters who need a home."

Ruth wiped her eyes on her handkerchief as Fred started the engine. "Not as good as Monty," she said.

CHAPTER 16

Matt's days crept slowly by. He missed Mom and Bonnie and Pookie. He wondered where Mom and Bonnie were now—in a graveyard someplace? He cried himself to sleep every night.

Denny placed and received calls all day long and late into the night. He said things like, "Two grand on Dandy Dancer to show," or "Five hundred on Bradshaw in seven."

Grandma and Grandpa didn't call.

Some days Denny was wildly happy, singing and urging Matt to play with his new toys; other days Denny practically snapped Matt's head off for walking through the room.

On one of the good days, he brought Matt a tennis

ball, then had a fit when Matt threw it against the back of the couch. He said the thump of the ball on the couch got on his nerves.

He often left Matt alone but never for more than an hour or so. When Denny was gone, Matt always practiced his pitching by throwing the tennis ball as hard as he could at the back of the couch, over and over. Matt wished he could be outside at home, throwing against the garage door. Better yet, he'd like to practice again with a real baseball, pitching to Bonnie.

One day when Denny was laughing and excited, he asked Matt what he'd like to do. "Something special," Denny said. "Something you always wanted to do. Ride to the top of the Space Needle? Visit the zoo?"

Matt didn't have to think long. "I want to go to a Mariners baseball game," he said.

Denny thought for a moment. "You got it," he said. When he came home that afternoon, he showed Matt two tickets. "We're going Saturday afternoon," he said. "After the game, we'll take the ferry to Bainbridge. You're going to meet your Uncle Winston, your Aunt Celia, and your cousins, Thomas and Tim."

"I have cousins?"

"Two boys, your age. Their house is right on the beach; we'll stay there overnight."

For the first time since he'd learned about Mom and

Bonnie's accident, Matt felt a glimmer of happiness. He was going to a game at Safeco Field! He was going to a sleepover with two boys his own age. He would take his new mitt; maybe the boys liked to play catch. Maybe he would even snag a fly ball at the game.

As the week wore on, Denny's crabby times came more and more often. On Friday afternoon he put all the movies and the DVD player in a big box. He put Matt's new baseball glove and the Walkman in the box, too.

"What are you doing?" Matt asked.

"Taking these back. They're no good."

"What's wrong with them? I haven't even caught a ball in the mitt yet. I'm going to take it to the ball game tomorrow."

"Don't argue with me! I'm returning all this stuff and getting a refund." Denny's eyes flashed with anger as he stomped about. He unplugged the PlayStation and grabbed all the video games, tossing them in the box.

Matt said no more. He had quickly learned not to talk during Denny's bad moods. He knew Denny didn't like him any more than he liked Denny, and sometimes Denny acted furious with him for no reason. Most of the time Matt felt as if Denny wished Matt were any place except in his apartment.

Denny had not hurt Matt, but Matt sensed that it could happen. Denny's anger flared easily, and Matt knew Denny always carried the small handgun he'd shown Matt in the car. The gun made Matt uneasy even though Denny never mentioned it.

Mom had warned Matt about guns. "Never pick one up," she told him. "If a friend shows you a gun, leave. Call me, and I'll come to get you."

Mom wouldn't like Matt living with someone who took a gun everywhere, but Mom wasn't here to object. He couldn't call her; she couldn't come to take Matt home.

"I'll be back in a little while," Denny said. He carried the box out, slamming the door behind him.

Matt looked around the room. He didn't care about losing the movies; he hadn't liked most of them anyway. Instead of animated Disney films and other G-rated movies, Denny had bought movies with lots of fighting and killing and car crashes. Matt covered his eyes during the car-crash scenes; they made him think about the wreck that killed Mom and Bonnie.

He didn't mind losing the PlayStation, either. It frustrated him because he couldn't read the directions, and Denny never took time to show him how to play. When Matt tried to do the games on his own, he didn't get far; he suspected they were intended for people older than six.

None of the board games had been opened because Denny wouldn't play them with Matt, and it was no fun alone.

He wished he could have kept the baseball mitt, though. He had worn it when he practiced pitching. When Denny was home and Matt couldn't throw the ball, he still kept the mitt on his hand for hours, pretending to pitch for the Mariners. He had planned to take it with him to the game tomorrow.

A new worry seized Matt. What if Denny returned the baseball tickets, too? What if they didn't take the ferry to the beach house tomorrow?

Matt went into Denny's bedroom and looked on the dresser top, where he had seen Denny drop the tickets. Lottery tickets with their numbers scratched off littered the dresser. He saw no baseball tickets.

Matt decided if Denny didn't take him to the ball game, he would run away.

I can't run away without money for food, Matt thought. He dragged a chair over to the refrigerator, climbed up, and opened the freezer section. I won't take all the money, he decided. If I only take part, he might not notice it's gone.

He listened for the front door to click open as he

took out the ice-cream carton and started prying off the lid. He didn't want to think about what would happen if Denny came back and caught him stealing money.

When the lid popped off, it slipped out of his hands and dropped to the floor. Matt scrambled off the chair, grabbed the lid, and looked inside the carton. Empty!

Matt climbed back on the chair and looked in the freezer, thinking he'd opened the wrong ice-cream container, but it was the only one.

He couldn't believe it! A few days ago, Denny had put a thick stack of money in here. What had happened to all of it?

This explained why Denny took all the toys back; he needed the money he'd paid for them.

Matt replaced the empty carton in the freezer and returned the chair. He couldn't run away when he didn't have any money. He'd starve.

Matt sat on the couch and played the list game. He closed his eyes and tried to remember everything he could about his mother and his sister and his dog.

He said the lists to himself every night before he went to sleep. He had made up lists of the stories Mom had read to him, the songs she sang, her clothes. He had one list of all the games Bonnie played with him. His favorite was when she pretended to be a catcher and he was a pitcher who threw fastballs.

"Ninety-eight miles an hour," Bonnie would say when she caught a ball. "Another zinger!" It used to make him laugh, but remembering made him sad. He always ended up crying when he played the list game, but he knew it was important not to forget his family.

Mom liked flowers, Matt thought, and music. She taught me the words to lots of songs like "Down by the Station, Early in the Morning" and "I've Been Working on the Railroad." She liked to drink tea and do cross-stitch. Best of all, she liked to have Matt sit on her lap while she read *Little Bear* or *Officer Buckle and Gloria* or *Blueberries for Sal* to him.

Bonnie liked to make beaded bracelets and run races with her track team and play her clarinet in the school band. She let Pookie sleep on her bed. Bonnie liked cinnamon rolls and ice cream.

Matt wished he hadn't eaten all the strawberry ice cream the last time they had it. If he had known Bonnie was going to be killed in a car wreck, he would have left the ice cream for her and not eaten a single spoonful.

Pookie's list was shorter: He liked to be petted, and he liked chew toys, and he liked to sleep in the sun.

Matt always put Pookie last in the list game because he hoped he might get Pookie back someday. Pookie wasn't killed in the crash. Maybe some nice people found Pookie at Marymoor Park, and someday Matt would see them walking him on a leash, and Matt would run to Pookie and hug him, and Pookie would be so excited and happy that the people would know he was really Matt's dog.

Denny returned, talking on the phone as he entered. He seemed calmer, but Matt pretended to be asleep.

Denny shook his shoulder. "I bought pizza," he said.

Matt opened his eyes and sniffed the cheese-and-tomato smell. "You said we couldn't afford pizza anymore."

"I got my money back for all those games. One clerk didn't want to give me a full refund on the opened movies, but I made such a stink, she caved in."

Matt was glad he hadn't been there. "Are we still going to the baseball game tomorrow?" he asked.

"I said we were going, didn't I?"

"I thought maybe you took the tickets back."

"I promised my kid we'd go to a ball game, and I always tell the truth. Besides, they're not refundable."

"And then we're going to ride the ferry and meet my cousins?"

"Your cousins and your aunt and uncle," Denny said. "There's only one thing."

"What?"

"You're going to have black hair and wear glasses tomorrow."

"I am? Why?"

"Because Thomas and Tim have dark hair, and they wear glasses. This is a family reunion and everybody's supposed to look alike for the pictures."

"Oh."

Denny opened a drawer and removed a small pair of eyeglasses with wire rims. "Here. Try them on."

Matt put the glasses on and looked through the lenses. "Everything looks the same," he said.

"It's clear glass. It won't change the way you see."

"How's my hair going to get black?"

Denny grinned. "Shoe polish. We'll do it in the morning."

The next morning Matt watched in the mirror as Denny applied black shoe polish to Matt's blond hair. Denny stroked it on slowly, careful not to get any color on Matt's ears or neck.

"This is how the movie stars get ready," Denny said.

Matt giggled. He looked so different, even Stanley wouldn't know him. When all his hair was black, Matt put on the glasses. "I don't look like me," he said. The red-and-gold Hawaiian-print shirt Denny had bought him was unlike anything in Matt's closet at home. Matt never chose shirts with buttons. He liked the new pants, though, with their deep pockets on both legs.

"Now all you need is a new name," Denny said.

"What's wrong with Matt?"

"Not a thing. But all the other kids have names that start with *T*—Thomas and Tim. You need a *T* name, too."

"For always?"

"You're going to be Travis."

Matt thought about that. "I'll be Travis for the weekend," he said. "Then I want to be Matt again."

He didn't understand why Denny wanted him to be exactly like his cousins. Mom had always said every person is unique and we should celebrate our differences, but Matt didn't say so. He didn't want to take any chance on making Denny angry today. Matt would have dyed his hair pink and called himself *Doofus* if that's what it took to go to a Mariners game, a ferry ride, and a sleepover with two other boys.

CHAPTER 17

Pookie slept with Bonnie Friday night. Even though he hogged the bed and snored, Bonnie wanted him where she could touch his fur anytime she felt like it.

Getting Pookie back had renewed her hope that Matt would come home, too. Of course she had never totally given up, but as the days went by, her optimism had faded.

The worst moment had come when she read on a Web site that seventy percent of abducted children who are murdered get killed within three hours of when they were taken. Three hours! Bonnie had cried, and that night she'd had the prairie dream again.

Now Pookie's familiar doggie smell comforted her as she lay in bed. For the first time since Matt's disappearance, she fell asleep quickly. She awoke once in the night because Pookie had a dream and his paws kept twitching against her side. Bonnie smiled as she talked to Pookie and petted him.

When Pookie went out his doggie door the next morning, Bonnie stood in the yard, too, even though it was raining. She knew the danger to Pookie was over, but she wasn't quite ready to let him be outside by himself.

She took the frayed brown "dog towel" from its hook and wiped Pookie's paws. Before she could rub down his back he shook vigorously, spraying droplets across the laundry-room floor.

As she came through the kitchen, she heard Mom on the telephone. "To be honest," Mom said, "we forgot all about it, but I agree it would be good for Bonnie to see her friends and do something fun. Hold on; let me ask her."

She held the phone away from her mouth. "It's Nancy's mom," she said. "She wants to know if she can pick you up for the baseball game."

"The Mariners game is today?"

"It starts at one o'clock. Mrs. Tagg is driving Shelly and Kristi—and Nancy, of course. She can pick you up at eleven."

"It doesn't seem right for me to go off to a Mariners game when Matt is still missing."

"I know, honey," her mother said, "but there's nothing more you can do to help Matt today, and we already bought your ticket. I think you should go."

"All right. I'll go." How odd, Bonnie thought, that I forgot about the Mariners game. When her track coach had arranged to get tickets at the group price, Bonnie had been thrilled. She had never seen a game at Safeco Field, and it would be great to go with her team-mates—thirty-four girls plus the coach and two parents.

"How could I have forgotten about something that seemed like such a big deal?" Bonnie asked her grandma.

"Because losing your brother is a bigger deal," Grandma said. "But I'm glad you're going, honey. You've done everything you can to help Matt. It's time you let your life start again."

"Catch a fly ball for me," Grandpa said. Then he gave Bonnie twenty dollars for a hot dog or cotton candy or whatever she wanted to buy at the game.

"Thanks, Grandpa."

"I wish I could go with you," he said. "I'll watch the game on television and think about you. Wave if you see a TV camera."

Mom insisted Bonnie take their bird-watching binoculars. "It's fun to see the players up close," she said.

When Bonnie first got in the van with her friends, she felt awkward, as if she'd been away far longer than a week. But when she told them about getting Pookie back, everyone cheered and asked lots of questions. Bonnie relaxed. The other girls told her what had happened at school that week and then they all sang "Take Me Out to the Ball Game," at the top of their lungs.

By the time Mrs. Tagg parked, the morning's drizzle had stopped. They strolled past outdoor stands selling peanuts, T-shirts, Cracker Jacks, hot dogs, and various souvenirs. The smell of grilled sausages tempted Bonnie, but she decided to wait and spend her money inside.

They walked alongside Safeco Field, admiring the huge pictures of the players on the outer walls of the stadium. Crowds lined up at the gates. Two people held up hand-lettered signs: NEED TICKETS.

"Programs!" called out a man on the corner. "Get your official souvenir programs!"

The girls posed in front of a sculpture of a huge baseball glove while Nancy's mom took their picture.

Mrs. Tagg cautioned them to keep their ticket stubs

so they could easily find their seats again if they needed to leave during the game. As soon as she went through the turnstile, Bonnie tucked her stub in her jeans pocket. She didn't plan to miss any of the game, though. She intended to watch every second of her first major-league baseball game.

They rode the escalator to the three-hundred level. Most of the girls bought something to eat before they found their seats, but Bonnie was too excited to feel hungry.

Her first glimpse of the field took her breath away. Green grass, mowed so it created a pattern; crisp white lines around the batter's box and along the baselines; a huge lighted scoreboard. It looked even better than it did on TV.

Vendors moved up and down the aisles hawking cotton candy, soft drinks, beer, and frozen malts. The peanut man used gestures to communicate with fans several rows away, then expertly flipped the bags of peanuts over his shoulder to the waiting customers. Money passed from person to person until it reached the vendors.

From their seats on the first-base side, the girls had a view of the Mariners' dugout. Bonnie aimed her binoculars at the players.

The retractable roof was closed because of the rain earlier in the day, but after the girls settled in their seats, the clouds blew away and the roof began to open.

Bonnie laughed as she recognized the music being broadcast: "Let the Sun Shine In." She watched the huge roof slide into itself on its track until blue sky covered the playing field. She would have to tell Grandpa how it worked. He liked mechanical things, and that roof was amazing.

It felt good to be with her friends and to think about something besides her brother. Then she felt guilty for having fun at Safeco Field when Matt, who loved baseball more than anything, was still missing.

What if he's never found? Bonnie thought. For the rest of my life, will I feel ashamed every time I start to enjoy myself?

She pushed the gloomy thought away, turned to Nancy, and said, "I hope the Mariners hit a home run today."

Matt sat on the kitchen floor, watching the digital clock on the oven. Denny had promised they would leave for the ballpark at eleven, and as eleven o'clock passed and then eleven-thirty, Matt's disappointment grew. He wanted to see batting practice. He wanted to walk around Safeco Field and look at all the souvenir stands before the game began.

Denny kept making phone calls and checking things on the computer as the clock numbers flashed toward noon. Matt grew more and more nervous that they wouldn't get to the game at all.

When Denny finally said, "Let's go," Matt rushed to the car, forgetting to put on the glasses. Denny made him go back to get them.

By the time they got to Safeco Field, all the parking places on the street were already taken. Denny got angry at the fees charged by the parking lots.

"That's highway robbery," he said. "Fifteen bucks to let my car sit for a couple of hours. I have half a mind to go back home. You can watch the game on television."

"We already have the tickets," Matt said.

Denny drove farther and farther away from the stadium, looking for a free parking spot. He didn't find one, so he parked in front of a business with NO STADIUM PARKING signs posted on the building. A few other cars had parked there, too. "I'll take my chances," Denny said. "They can't tow everybody."

As they approached Safeco Field, Matt heard "The Star-Spangled Banner" being sung. He walked faster. "We're going to miss the first pitch."

"There'll be plenty of other pitches."

Inside the stadium, Denny led the way through crowds of people buying refreshments. Although Matt wished he could have popcorn or an ice cream, he didn't ask for any because he didn't want to wait. Overhead television monitors showed the game had already begun.

Their seats were on the second level, past third base toward the outfield. By the time Denny found the correct aisle and then their row, the Mariners were up to bat in the bottom of the first.

In the second inning, Denny's phone rang. When he began talking loudly, people nearby gave him annoyed looks until he walked up the aisle to have his conversation on the concourse.

He didn't return until the third inning. Matt hoped he would stay this time. It was more fun to watch a ball game *with* someone, even his dad, who didn't care about baseball.

The girls sitting on the other side of Matt giggled and acted rowdy; they paid no attention to Matt or the Mariners.

The cotton-candy vendor walked past. Matt wished Denny would offer to buy some, but he didn't.

Denny left for another phone call in the fifth inning and stayed away so long, Matt grew nervous. One part of him cheered for the Mariners while another part worried about Denny.

What if Denny came back in one of his angry moods? He might want to leave before the seventh-inning stretch when the Mariner Moose drove his quad around the field. Stanley had told Matt about that, and Matt really wanted to see the Moose do it.

Matt had figured out that Denny's phone calls always involved winning or losing money. When Denny won, he was happy. He ordered pizza and bought Matt new toys. When Denny lost, he got angry and nothing Matt did pleased him. The last two days, Denny must have lost a lot. Matt remembered the empty ice-cream carton.

He looked anxiously down the aisle. What if Denny didn't come back? He didn't like living with Denny, but at least Denny gave him a place to sleep and food to eat. Without Denny, Matt might end up like the homeless man he'd once seen standing beside the freeway exit, holding a sign—HUNGRY. NEED MONEY FOR FOOD.

Mom had told him if he was ever in trouble to tell his phone number to a police officer or other adult, but she had also said, "Don't talk to strangers." The only police Matt saw were down on the field, where fans weren't allowed, and Matt didn't see any adults he knew. Besides, his phone number wasn't any good now that nobody lived in his house.

Matt nervously fingered one ear, pulling on the earlobe.

Bonnie stood at the entrance to her section, waiting for Nancy. Between innings, they had gone to the restroom together and then to a souvenir stand, where Bonnie bought a Mariners baseball. Now Nancy wanted to buy some nachos.

"I'll wait for you where I can see the game," Bonnie had said when she saw the long line at the food stand. "I want to watch the Mariners bat."

She pointed her binoculars at the Mariners on-deck circle. Mom was right; it was fun to see the players up close. She watched the first baseman walk to the plate, then smack the ball on the first pitch and send it sailing high into the second-deck stands beyond third base.

Bonnie followed the foul ball with her binoculars. Half a dozen fans scrambled to catch it. One of them spilled his drink all over the woman in front of him as he lunged for the ball.

Bonnie chuckled as she watched the successful fan hold the ball in the air while his friends cheered.

She scanned the crowd around the man with the ball. As she moved the binoculars from left to right, she suddenly stopped and reversed direction.

She stared at a boy who was pulling on his earlobe, exactly the way Matt always did when he was nervous. Bonnie's scalp prickled as she blinked and adjusted the focus. The boy was Matt's size, but he had black hair and he wore glasses. He had on a gaudy shirt with buttons up the front; Matt disliked buttons and wore only pullover shirts.

She didn't think the boy was Matt, but there *was* a resemblance, especially around the eyes. Detective Morrison had said whoever took Matt might change his appearance.

Bonnie looked to see who sat next to the boy. There was an empty seat on one side of him. On the other side, a pair of teenage girls jumped and danced as they held up a sign, clearly hoping the fan camera would put their picture on the big screen. Behind the boy, a young couple with a sleeping baby ate hot dogs.

It can't be Matt, Bonnie thought. Nobody was making that boy sit there by himself. If Matt had been left alone at Safeco Field, he wouldn't sit calmly and watch the baseball game. He would tell an usher or the parents of those girls sitting beside him who he was. He'd say he had been abducted and needed help. He would give an adult his phone number and have them call Mom or ask someone to call the police.

Bonnie let the binoculars dangle from the strap. A train whistle filled the air as a train passed Safeco Field. Bonnie tried to concentrate on the batter.

The boy only looks like Matt because I'm thinking so much about him, Bonnie told herself. She remembered riding in the country last summer. Each time she saw a DEER CROSSING sign, she looked so hard for deer that she imagined every large rock or tree stump was a buck or doe.

Was it going to be like that with Matt? Every time she saw a boy Matt's size, would she imagine it was him whether it made sense or not?

Still . . .

She peered through the binoculars once more. The boy kept pulling on his ear. Bonnie decided to go closer and then look again. She moved the binoculars until she saw which section the boy sat in. She turned and walked down to the concourse.

She didn't want to tell Nancy or the rest of her group where she was going; no point getting everyone all excited when she was sure it couldn't really be Matt.

She found Nancy still waiting in line for her nachos, and said, "I saw a friend of my mom's, and I'm going to go talk to him for a few minutes. I'll see you back at our seats."

Then she went down to the second level and walked as fast as she could around the concourse until she reached the third-base side of Safeco Field.

CHAPTER 18

Denny pressed the phone to one ear and covered his other ear with his hand, straining to hear through the crowd noise.

"Bronco tells me you paid him."

Denny recognized Hank's voice; his stomach did somersaults.

"Right," Denny said. "Right! And I'll pay you, too."

"Today." Even with the noise around him, Denny caught the threat in that one word.

"I can't get the money out of the bank until Monday," Denny said. "I'll pay you then."

"I've heard that before."

"I'm not stringing you along, Hank, I swear. I'll bring your money first thing Monday morning."

"I'll probably regret this," Hank said, "but you have until Monday noon. After that, no excuses."

"I'll be there," Denny promised. He put the phone in his pocket and paced nervously. Winston and Celia were his only hope, but the last time Denny had tried to borrow from them, Winston had said, "Get yourself some help for your problems first. Stop gambling, and learn how to get along with people so you can hold a job."

Denny had sworn he would do so even though he knew he didn't have any problem. He could quit gambling anytime he wanted to; he'd had a string of bad luck, that's all, and the only people he didn't get along with were the jerks of the world, who seemed to be everywhere. They had the problem, not him.

Celia and Winston often urged Denny to "get some professional help." Once, after Denny threatened to shoot a driver who cut him off in traffic, Celia had given him a phone number to call. "You need help to control your temper," Celia said, "before you hurt someone."

Denny's blood boiled as he remembered how Celia and Winston had jumped all over him when the other driver was at fault. Denny had thrown the number away.

It would be different today. Celia and Winston would be sympathetic when they found out Denny needed the money for Matt. They knew how much it costs to raise kids.

He'd say he needed it to buy clothes and a bed for Matt. He'd say he had custody of the boy and needed cash to take Matt to the doctor and to buy allergy medicine. He'd say he had an interview next week for a real job with a steady paycheck because more than anything he wanted to take good care of his boy.

They'd agree to help this time instead of lecturing Denny to change his ways.

But what if they didn't? What if Winston and Celia said no? What if Celia threw a fit because Denny had never paid back the last loan? What if they had somehow found out about his time in prison?

Hank and his partner could get mean. If Denny didn't come up with the cash by Monday, he would have to hide out for a while. The money from the merchandise he'd returned wasn't nearly enough to pay off Hank, and he'd already spent part of it on Lotto tickets.

He watched people buying refreshments, then read the posted prices. Six bucks for a beer! Cash flowed all around him, but Denny's pockets were nearly empty.

He had to get enough money from Winston and

Celia not only to pay off Hank but also to place some bets on next week's races. He had a hot tip on one race; he'd have big bucks soon. Winning felt better than anything else in the world.

He fidgeted, watching the people, resenting the easy way they purchased hot dogs and drinks. Why should foolish fans in baseball caps be able to afford what he could not?

He itched to talk to Winston and Celia, hit them up for a loan, and tuck the check safely in his pocket.

When he got home tomorrow, Denny would prepare to move. His rent was already a week overdue; he had to leave before the landlord came to collect. Children weren't allowed in the complex; the landlord would notice Matt.

He'd pay Hank Monday morning, then hit the road. The money from Winston and Celia would give him a fresh start. Maybe he and Matt would go back to Reno, where the gambling was good.

A new idea struck him. He could say Matt needs surgery and there's no insurance on him. Surgery is expensive; at least ten thousand dollars. With that much money, he and Matt could fly to Reno. He'd use one of his fake IDs for the plane.

Excited by this surefire plan, Denny rushed back to his seat. They would leave right now, catch an earlier ferry, and give Winston and Celia more time to get over their shock about Matt before Denny asked for the money.

Denny sat beside Matt and said, "Come on, kid. We're going."

"Now? The bases are loaded and the game is tied."

"We have to catch the ferry. Let's go."

Reluctantly Matt stood and followed Denny. Just then Matt heard a sharp *crack!* as the bat hit the baseball. A grand slam!

The crowd exploded. Matt cheered and clapped as he watched the players round the bases.

"Quit stalling!" Denny grabbed Matt's arm and pulled him along.

Don't get your hopes up, Bonnie told herself. This isn't a mystery novel. You aren't the brilliant girl detective who saves her brother from the crook.

She walked as fast as she could, dodging fans carrying cardboard trays full of food. The concourse was so crowded she wondered if anyone was still watching the game until a huge roar arose from the stadium.

From the television monitor, she heard Dave Niehaus, the Mariners announcer, shout, "Get out the rye bread and mustard, Grandma. It's grand salami time!"

A grand slam! The crowd was going crazy. The first Mariners game of my life, Bonnie thought, and I'm missing the best part, because I'm on a wild-goose chase after a kid with black hair and glasses who looks a little bit like my brother.

But she didn't turn back.

When she was one aisle from where the boy had been sitting, she decided she was close enough to get a really good look at him without actually confronting him. She walked up to the seating area and turned her binoculars toward the seats one section to her left. She moved them back and forth, but didn't find the boy.

She scanned the crowd again, more slowly, and saw the two girls who had sat beside the boy. The girls were still jumping and screaming. This time there were two empty seats beside them. The boy was gone.

Maybe he's using the restroom, Bonnie thought. She returned to the concourse area and looked in both directions, but it was hard to spot a small boy amid so many adults.

Bonnie hesitated. Should she go talk to those girls—ask them if the boy had told them his name? Little kids are friendly; he might have talked to them.

Of course if Matt had dyed hair and glasses and new clothes, he probably had a different name as well. Whoever had taken him wouldn't let him use the name

Matt Sholter anymore. But Matt would never go along with such a pretense unless his abductor was there with him, making him pretend to be someone else. Nobody had been forcing that boy to do anything.

I should forget it, Bonnie thought. I saw a kid pulling on his ear the way Matt does, and I got all excited, but it wasn't him, so I need to return to my own seat before Nancy's mother worries about me. Probably lots of kids pull on their ears. It's a habit, like nail biting or knuckle cracking.

She started back toward the first-base side. As she walked past the escalator that leads to the street, she glanced down. On the moving steps one flight below, she saw the black-haired boy, riding down. Directly behind him was Denny Thurman.

Shock zapped through every nerve in Bonnie's body. She recognized Denny immediately, even though she had not seen him since she was seven. It *is* Matt, Bonnie thought. Detective Morrison was right; Matt's dad took him!

Bonnie clutched the escalator railing, feeling the smooth rubber slide beneath her hands while her heart beat *rat-a-tat-tat*, like the snare drum in a marching band. She had only a moment to decide: run to a phone and call the police—or follow Matt and Denny down the escalator.

What if Denny had parked in the lot directly across from the stadium? Or on the street only a block or two away? He and Matt could be in a car and gone before the police found them.

Bonnie stepped on the escalator.

Much as she longed to shout "Matt!" and rush down the escalator to hug her brother, Bonnie stood still, riding down quietly. Because Matt wasn't trying to escape, Bonnie assumed Denny had somehow threatened him if he ran or called for help.

She didn't want to endanger Matt. All she wanted to do was keep Denny and Matt in sight long enough to get a car license number, or if Denny and Matt got on a bus, she would get the bus number. Then she would call the police, and they would find the car or be waiting when Denny got off the bus.

Matt and Denny stepped off the escalator on the ground floor and headed toward the exit.

Bonnie easily kept Denny and Matt in view because few people were leaving the game early. Why would they, when the Mariners had come from behind with a grand slam?

Matt stopped to tie his shoelace. When he straightened up, he looked around, wanting one last look at Safeco Field. Even though he had to leave before the game ended, it had been exciting. He had especially liked seeing the Moose dance on the dugout, and the computer hydroplane race on the big screen, and, most of all, the Mariners' grand slam. Maybe he could come again sometime; maybe next time Denny would sit with him and watch the action, and they could stay to see the Moose ride around the field. Maybe he would get another mitt.

Matt heard the crowd yelling again. He glanced at the escalator and found himself staring up at his sister. He blinked and looked again. His whole face lit up.

"Bonnie!" he shouted. He pointed up at her. "Look, it's Bonnie!" He waved his hands over his head, jumping with excitement.

Denny whirled around. His eyes met Bonnie's, and his face froze into a mask of fear and hatred.

Bonnie turned and began running back up the down escalator.

She heard Matt's panicked shout, "Don't leave me!"

Bonnie stopped, remembering what the court psychiatrist had told Detective Morrison about Denny: *He doesn't care who he hurts as long as he gets what he wants.* What would Denny do if she ran? She couldn't leave Matt alone with him while she sought help.

Bonnie turned back, feeling trapped as the escalator carried her closer to Denny and Matt.

When she stepped off the escalator, Matt flung his

arms around her. "You're alive!" he cried. "You didn't die in the accident."

She held him close. Despite her anger at Denny, tears of joy stung her eyes. Matt was okay.

Then his words sank in. "What accident?" she asked. "Of course I'm alive." As she looked over the top of Matt's black hair, she saw Denny unzip his sweatshirt partway, then slip his hand inside.

"I have a gun," he said softly. "Say one word to anyone, and your brother will be dead."

Bonnie clutched Matt and stared at Denny. "If you shoot a gun here, you'll never get away," she said. "A thousand people will hear it go off."

"Wrong," he said. "I have a silencer on it."

Bonnie assumed that meant the gun wouldn't make noise when it was fired.

"I have plans for Matt today," Denny said, "and if you want him to live, you'll help me keep them."

"What are the plans?"

"You don't need to know. Just do what I tell you to do."

Still clinging to Matt, Bonnie nodded agreement.

"The two of you are going to walk out of this stadium in front of me," Denny said. "You won't talk to anyone or try to signal for help or do anything to suggest we are not a happy family."

"He does have a gun," Matt whispered. "He wears it on a strap across his chest."

Bonnie wondered how Denny had made it through the security check at the gate with a handgun under his sweatshirt. Mrs. Tagg's tote bag full of peanuts and granola bars had been thoroughly searched and her water bottle confiscated. Well, it didn't matter how he'd smuggled a gun into the ball game. What mattered was preventing him from using it.

She put her hand on Matt's shoulder and walked with him toward the exit. Denny Thurman stayed directly behind them.

"What about Mom?" Matt asked. "Is she alive, too? Did she get well after the accident?"

"Mom wasn't in an accident."

"She wasn't? Denny talked to Mrs. Watson and she said—"

"Be quiet!" Denny said angrily.

Bonnie looked at her brother's face, glowing with happiness, and understood why he had sat alone in the crowd without asking for help and why he had never called home. Denny must have told Matt that she and Mom had been killed. Even though they were in terrible trouble, Matt looked happy because this danger mattered less to him than learning his mother and sister were alive.

Poor Matt, she thought. He must have felt so sad and alone. She wondered if he had nightmares.

They exited the stadium near the sculpture of the baseball mitt, where Bonnie and her friends had posed for a picture. They walked past the stadium to the corner where a motorcycle policeman was ready to direct traffic at the end of the game. A few other people stood on the curb, waiting to cross the street.

Bonnie stared at the police officer, willing him to look her way. *This is Matt!* she wanted to shout. *This is the boy who's been missing! Help us!*

"Don't say a word," Denny whispered.

Bonnie tried to make eye contact with the officer, but he only blew his whistle and waved for the people to cross the street.

The wind picked up and dark clouds covered the sun again. Bonnie buttoned her coat.

As they stepped off the curb, Bonnie reached for Matt's hand. For the last few months he had objected when Mom or Bonnie tried to take his hand, claiming, "I'm not a baby anymore. I know to watch for cars."

Today he slipped his hand quickly into Bonnie's. His warm fingers intertwined with hers, and when they reached the other side of the street, neither Bonnie nor Matt let go.

By the time they'd walked a few blocks, the other

pedestrians had turned up a side street or had reached their cars and driven away. Denny, Matt, and Bonnie kept walking. Bonnie wondered if they were headed for a car or if Denny lived in downtown Seattle and was taking her home with him.

"I have to go to the bathroom," Matt said.

"Not now," Denny said.

"Now," Matt insisted.

"You'll have to wait. The car's only a few more blocks."

"I can't wait. I have to go bad."

Bonnie's thoughts raced faster than the traffic speeding along the freeway behind them. We need to be where people will notice us, she thought. Taking Matt to the bathroom might be their only chance to get help.

"There's a restaurant across the street," Bonnie said. "He could use the bathroom there."

Denny stopped walking, as if he were thinking it over.

"I have to go bad," Matt said.

"You wouldn't want him to make a mess in your car," Bonnie said.

"I wouldn't . . ." Matt began, but Bonnie squeezed his hand hard, and he didn't finish the sentence.

"Okay," Denny said. "Okay, we'll go in the restaurant, but remember what will happen if you say anything. I'll do the talking." He led the way across the street.

A banner over the restaurant door said WELCOME MYSTERY FANS! Inside, every table was full; people laughed and talked. A waiter in a white jacket with a stethoscope hanging around his neck walked past carrying a tray of drinks.

A woman in a long red evening gown, a rhinestone tiara, and a gold streamer across her chest that said MISS CLUELESS, asked, "Are you here for the mystery meal?"

"No," Denny said. "My son is desperate to use a bathroom."

The woman smiled. "Sure. The men's room is that way." She pointed.

"Make it fast," Denny said, "and don't talk to anybody."

"You'd better take him," Miss Clueless said.

"He can go by himself," Denny said. "We'll wait here."

Bonnie knew Denny didn't trust her. He was afraid if he went into the restroom with Matt, Bonnie would ask for help, and he was right.

"You should go with him," the woman urged. "We're having a solve-the-mystery party, and there are a lot of odd things happening." She leaned closer and whispered so none of her customers could hear. "There are two actors headed toward the men's room right now and they're going to stage a fake robbery. Your son would be terrified."

"I'll take him to the ladies' room," Bonnie said.

"I can't go in the girls' bathroom," Matt said.

"Yes, you can." She squeezed Matt's hand, holding her breath and hoping Denny would say yes. Maybe a customer would be in there, and Bonnie could tell the woman who she was. Someone in the restroom might even have a cell phone, and Bonnie could call the police.

Denny looked at Bonnie, his eyes narrow. "Come right back," he said, *"and don't talk to anyone."* He put his hand inside his sweatshirt as he spoke. "Do you understand?"

Bonnie nodded. She understood perfectly.

"Ladies' is right down the hall," said Miss Clueless.

Bonnie walked that way, with Matt beside her.

There was no one else in the restroom. Matt went in a stall.

Bonnie squirted liquid soap on her index finger and wrote on the mirror: *HELP!! Denny Thurman kidnapped*

That's as far as she got when the door opened and

two matronly women entered. Bonnie felt faint with relief.

"You have to help me," she told the women. "My brother was abducted, and now the man's making me go with him, too. He's out there right now waiting for us, and he has a gun." The words tumbled from her lips as she pleaded with the women. "Call the police! Tell them where we are. Tell them we're with Denny Thurman."

The two women smiled at each other, clearly delighted by what Bonnie said. "A clue in the ladies' room," one said. "I didn't expect that!"

"Let's go tell the boys," the other woman said. "We can freshen our makeup later."

"This isn't a clue!" Bonnie said. "This is real! Call the police!"

But the women, laughing, went back out. One spoke over her shoulder to Bonnie as they left. "You did a fine job, dear," she said, "and you're so young to be an actress!"

CHAPTER 19

Bonnie's hand shook with frustration as she finished writing her soapy message on the restroom mirror. *HELP!! Denny Thurman kidnapped Matt & Bonnie Sholter. Gun.*

She no longer believed any of the customers would take her plea seriously. Not today, when the restaurant was hosting a mystery meal where the diners try to solve a fake crime. Her only hope was for an actress to see the message and realize it wasn't part of the mystery script.

Behind her, Matt came out of the stall.

"Why didn't you back me up?" Bonnie demanded. "Why didn't you tell those women I wasn't acting?"

Matt look embarrassed. "I didn't want anyone to

see me in the girls' bathroom." He pointed at the wall behind Bonnie. "Let's climb out the window," he said.

Bonnie eyed the window—a narrow rectangle of frosted glass high on the wall above a radiator—and wondered if she could squeeze through it.

"It's worth a try," she said. She climbed on the radiator, reached up, and turned the window latch. When she pushed on the window frame, the bottom moved outward.

The opening was only about a foot wide. Matt could probably get through it, but she wasn't sure she would fit.

"You first," she said as Matt scrambled up and stood beside her on the radiator.

She bent over, with her hands on her knees. "Stand on my back; I think you'll be able to reach the window."

Matt climbed on Bonnie's back, then stood up and grabbed the window frame.

"Hurry," she said. "You're heavy!"

Matt swung one leg up and through the opening, then the other leg. He slid down the outside of the building and dangled for a moment, still grasping the ledge with both hands. "It isn't too far down," he said.

Rubbing her back, Bonnie straightened up. "Let go!" she said. "If I get stuck, don't wait for me. Run away! Get help."

He released his grip and dropped to the ground. "I'm okay," he called. "You can do it, too, Bonnie. You'll fit."

Quickly Bonnie pulled herself up. By sucking in her breath and scraping her back on the top of the opening, she squeezed through. She dropped down beside Matt.

They stood beside three garbage cans in a short, narrow alley on the back side of the restaurant. At the end of the alley, cars drove past on the street that ran along the side of the building.

"We could hide in the garbage cans," Matt said.

Bonnie shook her head. "Let's run for it," she said. "We'll flag down a car and get help."

Together the children bolted toward the street.

Parked vehicles lined the curb. Bonnie and Matt stepped between two parked cars into the street, then waved frantically at an approaching white Toyota.

The Toyota's driver frowned at them and kept going.

Denny paced nervously back and forth beside the hostess station. What was taking those kids so long? They should have been back by now.

The noise level in the restaurant continued to increase. A man rushed out of the restroom claiming he had been robbed at gunpoint, which put the whole place in an uproar. Denny's head started to ache.

When Miss Clueless returned, Denny said, "My kids haven't come out of the restroom. Could you check to see if they're all right?"

Miss Clueless, looking annoyed, headed for the ladies' bathroom. Instead of going all the way in, she opened the door, poked her head in the anteroom, and called, "Anybody here?" No one answered.

A few seconds later she returned. "They aren't in there," she said. "Maybe you missed them and they're waiting outside."

Denny put a hand on her arm. "Are you sure?"

"Of course I'm sure. If you don't believe me, go look for yourself. The ladies' room is empty." I'm too busy to babysit his kids, she thought. This guy wasn't even a paying customer.

Denny rushed past her down the hall and pushed open the door of the women's bathroom. As he stepped into the anteroom, a woman came toward him on her way out.

Denny stopped.

The woman screamed.

"Sorry," Denny said as he backed away.

"Peeping Tom!" the woman said. "For shame!"

"I'm looking for my kids," he said. "The hostess said nobody was in there."

"I can see why," she said. "It's freezing in here. I just came in, but it's too cold to use the facilities. The toilet seat would feel like an ice cube. If you're one of the actors, tell the manager to have someone close the window and turn on the heat."

Denny looked over the woman's shoulder at the open window. "No!" he said. He dashed out of the restroom, brushed Miss Clueless out of his way, and opened the door. He ran out, looked both directions, then raced to the corner, where he turned and ran alongside the building until he reached the alley. From there he could see the open window, but he did not see Matt and Bonnie. He ran down the alley toward the other street.

A dark green van came toward the frantic children.

"Help!" Bonnie shouted as she waved at the van. "We need help!"

The van stopped for a red light. The windows, both front and rear, went down and three teenage boys looked out.

"What's the problem?" the boy in the backseat asked.

"Take us with you," Bonnie said. "We'll explain after we get away from here."

The boys looked at one another.

"Please!" Bonnie said. "You have to help us."

The driver said, "We don't have to do anything. My old man would kill me if I picked up hitchhikers."

"They're kids," one of the other boys said. "Maybe they really need help."

"Maybe they're working the streets, and as soon as we unlock the doors, a gang of carjackers shows up and gets in with them."

"There's no gang," Bonnie said. "My brother's dad has a gun and he's making us go with him. Please, please, let us in! You don't have to take us far; drive us to the nearest police officer and we'll get out."

"There are cops all over, directing traffic," the boy in back said. "We'd only have to take them a few blocks."

"We don't have time to argue," Bonnie said. She tried to open the rear door of the van, but it was locked.

"Hey! You there!" Denny's voice came from behind them. "You leave my kids alone!"

Matt started to cry.

"He's trying to kidnap us," Bonnie told the boys. "He stole my brother, and now he's trying to take me, too."

Denny reached the van. "You young punks," he said. "I ought to turn you in to the cops, trying to lure children into your car."

"We didn't do anything," the driver said. "They waved for us to stop."

"You expect me to believe that?" Denny said. "I let my kids out of my sight for two minutes, and some pervert tries to snatch them."

"He's lying," Bonnie said. "If you won't help us, at least go tell the police what we told you. He abducted us."

"She's lying," Denny said. "She stole money from her teacher and now she's trying to run away."

The three boys gaped at Bonnie.

The light changed; the driver behind the van honked his horn.

"Get out of here before I decide to teach you a lesson," Denny snarled. "How would your parents react if you're arrested for trying to molest a child?"

The windows shot up.

The van sped away.

Bonnie's hope of getting rescued went with it.

Denny glared at her. "I told you not to talk to anyone."

Bonnie didn't answer. Beside her, Matt continued to cry softly.

Bonnie expected Denny to march them back to the other street where they had been walking, but instead he raised his hand and hailed a passing taxicab.

"Get in," he said.

"What about your car?" Matt asked.

"I'll get it tomorrow. We're going to miss the ferry if we waste any more time."

They piled into the backseat of the cab. Bonnie hoped the cabdriver would remember them later. When she didn't return to her seat at Safeco Field, she knew a huge police search would ensue. Maybe the cabbie would recall a crying boy and a scared girl and an angry-looking man. Maybe he would tell the police where he dropped them off, and what the man looked like.

Bonnie realized Denny looked nothing like the police sketch of the man suspected of taking Matt. That man had dark curly hair and a mustache; Denny was blond and clean-shaven. Bonnie wondered if he had a rose tattoo on his arm.

Heavy traffic blocked the streets. As the cab crept down First Avenue and idled at red lights, Bonnie tried to figure out how to escape. If only Denny didn't have a gun. She could have screamed in the stadium or run to the traffic cop or asked Miss Clueless to call for help. If Denny wasn't armed, she and Matt could even jump out of the cab right now, while it stopped at a red light.

But he did have a gun and he'd threatened to use it on Matt, so Bonnie kept silent and stayed in the taxi.

When they reached the ferry terminal, Bonnie slipped her hand in her pocket, withdrew her ticket stub from the ball game, and laid it on the seat. It wasn't the greatest clue in the world, but it was the best she could do. She hoped the driver cleaned out the cab after every fare.

Denny asked the cabdriver to wait.

"I'll have to leave the meter running," the driver said.

"No problem," Denny said.

"Aren't we going on the ferry?" Matt asked as they walked up the ramp beside a nonworking escalator.

"We're going," Denny said.

"Then why did you have the cabdriver wait?"

"So I didn't have to pay him. By the time he realizes we aren't coming back, we'll be gone."

What a mean trick, Bonnie thought.

In the terminal, Matt paused by a huge antique clock, but Denny said they didn't have time to look at it. He went straight to the ticket window and bought three tickets for Bainbridge Island.

"You barely made it," the ticket person said. "Walk-ons will start boarding at gate two in a few minutes."

As Denny paid for the tickets, Bonnie stood behind him and waved at the ticket seller to get her attention. When the woman looked at her, Bonnie mouthed the word *help*. She pointed at Denny, then made a "gun" with her thumb and pointer finger and pretended to shoot Matt.

The startled woman looked from Bonnie to Denny, then back at Bonnie. Bonnie quickly dropped her hand as Denny took his change. They continued past the ticket booth. As they walked away, Bonnie glanced once over her shoulder. The woman in the ticket booth stared after them.

Please, Bonnie thought. Please, please call the police and tell them which ferry we're on.

Denny draped his arm across Bonnie's shoulder, his fingers digging into her arm. "Smile," he said, under his breath. "Act happy."

Bonnie gritted her teeth and forced a smile.

"I wonder how long the cabbie will sit there," Denny said, "before he figures out we aren't coming back."

They joined the crowd waiting to board. College students chattered about their classes; one man had an assistance dog; a woman pushed a baby stroller.

A sign beside the door said ATTENTION in red letters. It warned people to report suspicious activity to any ferry worker.

I did, Bonnie thought. I warned the ticket seller.

She looked behind her and saw a man in uniform

cross the lobby near the big clock. The bright green vest that he wore over the uniform said SEATTLE POLICE.

Bonnie held her breath. Had the ticket seller called the police already? Was the officer coming to talk to her right now? She pretended to scratch her shoulder so she had a reason to keep looking back.

Instead of entering the room where ticketed passengers waited to board, the police officer stopped to chat with a man who was mopping the floor.

"Your attention please! Walk-on passengers to Bainbridge Island may now board at gate two."

Bonnie and Matt, with Denny at their heels, joined the crowd that filed down the ramp and on to the huge white-and-green ferry. In the middle of so many people, Bonnie felt all alone.

The last few cars drove aboard. Attendants in lime green vests with orange stripes directed the drivers where to park, and put blocks of wood in front of the tires of the cars nearest the front. Soon the ramp raised and the ferry backed away from the dock.

Denny took the first vacant bench seat and had Bonnie sit next to the window, with Matt in the middle next to Denny. He fidgeted and kept glancing around. After only a few moments, he said, "There are too many people in here. We're going down to the car deck."

They descended two flights of stairs, to the deck closest to the water. The ferry wasn't full; only half the parking spaces held cars, and they were all at the other end, facing the direction the ferry was going.

Gulls swooped beside the ferry, their raucous cries riding high over the noise of the engines and the churning water. Bonnie watched the Seattle skyline grow smaller as the ferry moved west.

Under other circumstances she would have enjoyed picking out Seattle landmarks: the Pacific Science Center, the Space Needle, the grain terminal. Huge orange cargo cranes, the kind used to load containers onto barges or freighters, stood guard all along the waterfront.

She could see the curved tops of Seahawk Stadium and Safeco Field. Was the Mariners game over yet? Were Nancy and her mother and the rest of the track team frantically searching for her?

I should never have followed Denny by myself, Bonnie thought.

I knew he was dangerous. What was I thinking? Instead of getting on the escalator, I should have run to the nearest concession booth and asked an adult to call the police. By the time Denny walked to his car, the police would have been there. Denny would be under arrest by this time and Matt would be on his way home.

Instead, Mom was probably getting a call right about now telling her Bonnie was missing, too. Poor Mom. She was already stressed-out, and so were Grandpa and Grandma. They would really fall apart over this latest development.

What am I going to do? Bonnie wondered. How can I get us out of this mess without being shot?

CHAPTER 20

Miss Clueless longed for the mystery to be solved so she could sit down. Her feet were killing her and this outfit made her look ridiculous, especially the banner with that stupid name on it.

On a normal day, she wore flat heels and a comfortable skirt and blouse to work, but for the Mystery Meals she always had to wear the red gown, the banner, and high heels. She worked harder, on these days, too. The Mystery Meals brought in crowds, so in addition to her hostess duties Miss Clueless helped clear the tables between courses.

As she piled dirty dishes on a tray, a pudgy woman with frizzy red hair tapped her on the shoulder.

"There's a message written on the mirror in the ladies' room," the redhead said. "It gives some names and says they've been kidnapped."

"Not again," said Miss Clueless.

"Since we're supposed to solve a murder, not a kidnapping, I thought I should tell someone, in case it's a real message."

"It's not real," Miss Clueless said. "Customers often plant phony evidence as a way to throw the others off track and give themselves a better chance to solve the mystery first."

"Oh," the redhead said. "That's a relief. I thought for a moment it was an actual plea for help."

"I'll take care of it," Miss Clueless said. She headed for the women's bathroom. Some people would do anything to solve the mystery and get their meal free.

The last time someone had left a fake clue on the mirror it was written with lipstick, and it had taken Miss Clueless fifteen minutes of hard work to get it off. Thank goodness whoever wrote this message had used soap.

She took a wad of wet paper towels and scrubbed away the words. The message came off easily.

She rubbed the mirror with dry towels and inspected her reflection. No trace of any soapy words.

She threw the towels in the trash container, then returned to the hostess station.

A cold wind blew across the open car deck, but Denny insisted they stay there.

"Where are we going?" Bonnie asked.

"We're going to meet our cousins," Matt said.

"We don't have any cousins."

"Yes, we do. Denny's sister has two boys my age, and we're going to stay overnight with them."

Bonnie realized Matt might have cousins she knew nothing about. Mom had told Detective Morrison that Denny had a sister.

"You have to call me Travis tonight," Matt said, "because all of the boys have names that start with *T*."

Bonnie gave Denny a disgusted look. "How are you going to explain us to your sister?" she asked.

"Matt—er, Travis is my son. That's all the explaining I need to do."

"No, it isn't. What about me? I'm not your child." To herself Bonnie added, *Thank goodness*.

Denny said nothing.

Anger spurred Bonnie on. "If your relatives have watched the television news this week or glanced at a newspaper, they will know Matt was abducted. Mom's been on every channel, pleading for his return."

"She has?" Matt said.

"She has, and her picture's been in all the papers." Bonnie looked at Denny. "Since you and Mom were once married, surely your sister would recognize Mom. Unless she's completely stupid, she'll put two and two together when you show up with Matt."

"Celia and Winston never met Anita. They lived back East, and we got married on the spur of the moment."

"Has *my* picture been in the paper?" Matt asked.

"Your picture is in store windows all over the state of Washington," Bonnie said. "It's in the newspapers and on TV. Your face is everywhere, including the Internet."

"Wow!" said Matt.

"He looks different now," Denny said. "No one will recognize him."

"I recognized him."

"You're his sister."

"I'll make a deal with you," she said.

Denny didn't respond.

Bonnie kept talking. "When we get to Bainbridge Island, you keep going, but let us reboard the ferry and go home. I promise we won't tell anyone where you are. You'll have a head start—a chance to get away."

"No way. You'd break your promise the minute I was out of sight."

"Suit yourself. Either you let us go home, or as soon as I see your sister, I'm telling her what happened. All of it. I don't think you'll shoot Matt or me in front of your sister and your nephews."

Bonnie hoped she sounded more confident than she felt. She knew it was risky to threaten Denny, but she didn't want to wait until she could ask Denny's sister for help. For all she knew, Denny's sister and brother-in-law were as bad as he was, and the two cousins were young punks on drugs. Denny's relatives might help him instead of helping her and Matt, even if they knew the truth.

"Celia won't believe you," Denny said. "I'm her brother. She knows I wouldn't lie to her."

Bonnie rubbed her hand across Matt's head, then showed Denny the streak of black on her palm. "It'll be easy to prove you dyed his hair," she said.

"Shut up!" Denny wiped his hand across his brow.

Bonnie couldn't keep quiet. He looked nervous; maybe she could convince him to let her and Matt go. "All your sister has to do is call the police. They'll verify everything I say."

Denny had never liked Bonnie when he was married to Anita, and he liked her even less now. How dare she interfere when he was on his way to Bainbridge with the perfect reason to ask for money. He was so close to pulling off his plan; he refused to let Bonnie spoil it.

He'd had an incredible losing streak since he took Matt. Eight days ago, he'd been riding high with more cash than he could stuff in his pockets. Now desperation chilled him more than the icy wind. Denny hated this feeling of impending disaster. He hated being broke, hated knowing the Hanks and Broncos of the world knew exactly how to track him down.

Even if his luck turned again so he could eventually afford to pay Hank, it would be too late. He'd be a marked man. He'd seen how Hank's anger worked: Pay up promptly or be the victim of a "hit-and-run accident" that wasn't an accident at all.

Denny needed money—*a lot* of money—and he needed it fast, before Monday morning. With Matt, he could get it. Without Matt, Denny was doomed to running from Hank and his henchmen.

His plan had worked fine until Bonnie showed up. Now this annoying girl with the big mouth threatened to ruin everything.

If he let Bonnie talk to Celia and Winston, he would never get the money he needed. Not only would they refuse to pay, they'd probably call the cops.

Denny could almost hear his righteous sister:

"You've gone too far this time, Denny. Kidnapping is a crime. I'm going to have to turn you in."

This time Denny would be in prison a lot longer than six months. The prosecutor would learn about Denny's previous conviction and his unregistered firearm. Denny couldn't afford a defense attorney. He'd be stuck with the public defender, who would treat him like scum and be secretly glad to lose the case.

Denny's head pounded. Tension headaches always made him sick, and now the up-and-down motion of the ferry increased his nausea.

He looked around. He and the two children were alone on the lower deck. The cars were empty; all the passengers had gone upstairs to the warm lounge area.

He glared at Bonnie. Loathing made his eyes narrow, as if by squinting at her he could make her disappear. Matt had agreed to do everything Denny said; why wouldn't the girl cooperate? She had wrecked it all.

Denny could think of only one solution. He had to get rid of Bonnie before the ferry docked.

Shove her overboard.

Pretend it was an accident.

Even if she screamed as she fell, no one would hear her cries over the noisy engine.

Wait. Denny took a deep breath and tried to think calmly.

What if Bonnie could swim? Other passengers might see the girl splashing in Puget Sound and call for help. The events played out in Denny's mind.

"Girl overboard!" the person would yell, and everyone would rush to that side of the boat to gawk.

The captain would stop the engine. Someone would throw Bonnie a life preserver and she'd hang on and get pulled back to the ferry, or some hero-type would dive in and keep her afloat until one of the small lifeboats could be launched to rescue her.

If Bonnie got plucked from the frigid water, the captain and crew and all the passengers would see a dripping-wet kid, shaking with cold, and hear her accuse Denny of kidnapping and attempted murder. She'd tell everything, *yak yak yak*, and Winston and Celia would see Denny on the nightly news as he was being led off to jail.

Denny cringed at the imagined scene. He couldn't let it happen. He refused!

I'll shoot her before I push her into the water, Denny thought. If she's dead, she'll sink right away.

CHAPTER 21

Detective Morrison dreaded this visit. How could she tell Anita Sholter that her daughter was missing? This was the hardest part of police work: breaking bad news to good people.

Detective Morrison and Spike had rushed to Safeco Field as soon as the call came in. A security guard, so upset he was barely coherent, had dialed 911 to report a girl had vanished from the ballpark.

At first Detective Morrison assumed it was a typical lost-child case and she wondered why Seattle Police were alerting her. Kids often get separated from the group they came with but usually they're reunited quickly, with no harm done. It's easy to get turned around in crowded places. Happens all the time.

Detective Morrison had been on her first break of a busy day when the call came, and her ham sandwich seemed more interesting than a kid who went out the wrong exit at the ballpark. She only half listened to the report—until she heard the name of the missing girl.

She concentrated on the words coming from the police radio: "This girl is the sister of six-year-old Matt Sholter, who vanished from his school eight days ago."

Detective Morrison dropped her sandwich and ran to her squad car. En route to Safeco with her siren screaming, she learned Bonnie had left her seat in the sixth inning and never returned.

When Detective Morrison arrived, she found a group of girls, plus a few adults, milling nervously around the private office of a Safeco Field official. She recognized Bonnie's pal, Nancy. Two Seattle Police Department officers were already questioning the group.

"Bonnie told me she saw someone she knew, a friend of her mom's," Nancy said. "She said she was going to talk to him and would meet me back at our seats, but she never came."

Someone she knew. Detective Morrison had wondered all along if the person who took Matt was someone he recognized—a family friend or a former neighbor, someone whom Matt would go with because he didn't consider the person to be "a stranger," as he'd been warned against. Had Bonnie now been lured by the same familiar person?

Detective Morrison felt sick to her stomach. Bonnie was a smart, capable girl. She would never willingly leave the ballpark, even with someone she knew, without first telling the people she had come with. It flat out would not happen. Which meant Bonnie had left against her will.

After questioning Bonnie's team and the chaperones, the three police officers left, each with an urgent assignment. Detective Morrison offered to do the worst task of all—inform Bonnie's mother—because she already knew Anita Sholter.

The rain began again as Detective Morrison drove out of downtown Seattle and headed east across the Mercer Island Bridge. By the time she stopped in front of the Sholter house, her mood matched the dismal weather.

With a heavy heart, Detective Morrison rang Anita Sholter's doorbell.

Mrs. Sholter took one look at the detective's face and knew she brought bad news. "Come in," she said.

"It's Bonnie. She told her friends she saw someone she recognized and would be back in a few minutes. She never returned."

The color drained from Mrs. Sholter's face. "Bonnie's gone?"

"She's missing. As soon as Seattle Police got the call, they ordered roadblocks around the whole district. They're checking every car in the parking garage. Those who parked on the street will be searched before they leave the area."

Mrs. Sholter nodded as if she understood, but Detective Morrison knew the woman was too shocked to pay full attention.

"Bonnie left the others during the bottom of the sixth inning," Detective Morrison continued. "They didn't report her missing until the game ended, nearly an hour later. Until then her group thought she was watching the game with the friend she'd seen. They didn't start to worry until the crowd began to thin out. Then they looked for her, and realized she wasn't coming back to her original seat."

"So Bonnie could have left the area before the road-blocks went up," Mrs. Sholter said.

"Correct."

"Do you think the same person who took Matt managed to take Bonnie?"

"We can't be sure, but it's awfully suspicious. It makes me wonder again if Matt recognized his abductor."

"If the same person was after Bonnie, he must have followed her to the Mariners game. How could some-one have stalked her like that? Where was Matt while this happened?"

Chills crept up Detective Morrison's arms. Was Matt dead and now the killer had come for Bonnie? Was this revenge on Mrs. Sholter by someone with a twisted mind and an old grudge?

"We don't know if Matt is still with his abductor," Detective Morrison said. Then, seeing Mrs. Sholter's stricken look, she added, "The kidnapper could have left Matt locked in somewhere, or had someone guard-ing him. Or maybe Matt was there. Maybe Bonnie saw him and followed him."

Bonnie's grandpa, who had listened to the whole conversation, said, "Perhaps the abductor used Matt as a decoy, to get Bonnie to go with him, the same way he used Pookie to trick Matt."

"You think Matt was at the ball game, in plain view of thousands of people?" Mrs. Sholter said. "Surely someone would have recognized him. Besides, if he had been out in public, he'd have screamed for help, and if Bonnie had seen him she would have called the police immediately."

Detective Morrison nodded. Mrs. Sholter was right. On the other hand, if Bonnie had not left the ballpark voluntarily, it meant she had been kidnapped. How could that happen to a thirteen-year-old girl in a crowded baseball stadium?

"Bonnie would never have left the game without consulting Mrs. Tagg," Mrs. Sholter said.

Detective Morrison knew this girl, knew this family, and she knew in her bones that Mrs. Sholter spoke the truth. Bonnie could be trusted to do the right thing.

What had happened? What in the world could have seemed so important to Bonnie that she would go against everything she'd been taught? Especially now, with her brother missing.

Grandpa said, "Whoever she went with had a weapon and forced her to leave the stadium."

Grandma said, "She wouldn't have gone otherwise."

Detective Morrison believed they were right. "There's no point speculating what happened," she said. "The important thing now is to find Bonnie as fast as possible. I'll need a picture of her."

It was like watching a rerun of a horrible movie where she stood in the Sholters' living room, asking for a photo of a missing child.

This time was worse because she knew the child personally. Knew her and liked her.

Throughout her nine years on the police force,

Detective Morrison had purposely maintained a detachment from the people she served. She knew if she let herself get emotionally involved in the cases she worked, she would burn out and not be able to continue.

Over the last week, however, Bonnie's loyalty to her brother and concern for her dog had touched Detective Morrison. The girl had distributed flyers, checked Web sites, knocked on doors, given interviews, and sent e-mails. She never gave up.

Bonnie Sholter was more than another missing person; she was a missing friend. When Mrs. Sholter handed over a picture of her daughter, her second child to vanish in eight days, Detective Morrison's heart broke for the woman.

No one should have to endure what this family was going through.

CHAPTER 22

The wind whipped Bonnie's hair around her face as Matt huddled against her. She slipped her hands in her jacket pockets to keep them warm, and found the souvenir baseball she'd bought at the Mariners game.

"Here," she said, handing the ball to Matt. "I bought you a present at Safeco Field."

Matt's eyes lit up when he saw the blue-and-green ball with the Mariners logo on it. He turned the ball carefully around and around in his hands. "Thanks," he said. He carried the baseball to a small patch of sunlight where the colors looked brighter.

Bonnie warily watched Denny, who stared at her as if she were his worst enemy. She wondered what he intended to do.

She knew she had angered him when she said his sister would believe her and not him. Even though it was true, Bonnie realized it might not have been smart to say so. She needed to keep him calm, not get him all worked up.

Denny stepped toward her, his hand inside his sweatshirt, presumably on the gun. When he was only about two feet away, he said, "You're going to walk as close to the edge as you can." He kept his voice low, but Bonnie saw Matt, who was now off to the side and behind Denny, stop examining the ball and pay attention.

"Why?" Bonnie asked. "What are you going to do?"

"I'm going to take my son to visit my sister and brother-in-law, without you there to interfere. Back up."

Bonnie stepped toward the rear of the ferry.

Matt, his eyes on Denny, began inching toward the stairway, but Denny looked over his shoulder and snapped, "You stay where you are and keep quiet or you won't live to meet your cousins."

Matt stopped.

Bonnie reached the yellow rope that stretched from side to side, preventing people from walking too close to the back edge of the boat. She looked at Denny.

"Duck under the rope and keep going."

Bonnie went under the rope. A few feet farther, a

strong mesh of rope blocked her from reaching the end of the ferry. She stopped with her back to the mesh.

"Climb over," Denny said. He now stood next to the yellow rope.

"I'm a strong swimmer," she said. "Even if you make me jump, I'll survive. Someone on the upper decks will hear me yell, and see me in the water."

"You won't be swimming," Denny said, "or yelling." His voice was hard as steel. His hand stayed inside his sweatshirt.

Beads of perspiration broke out on Bonnie's lip. She glanced at the stairs, hoping other passengers would come down to their cars, but no one came. The deck remained empty except for her, Denny, and Matt.

When she looked up, however, she saw two men watching through a window on the deck above. One of them pointed at her.

They see me, she thought. Even if they don't realize what's going on, they'll know I shouldn't be out here on the end of the boat. They'll tell a ferry worker, and someone will hurry down to make me get back where it's safe. I have to stall until that happens.

"Climb over the barrier," Denny said. "Now!"

Bonnie looked into his eyes and saw the face of a madman. He's going to fire the gun, she thought. As soon as I get to the edge of the deck, he's going to shoot me and let my body topple into the water.

Clyde Wallace and his brother, James, stood at the back end of the ferry's lounge, in the small outdoor smoking area. Through the window that shielded them from the wind, they looked down at the rear of the ferry.

"Hey!" James said. "Look at that girl down there. She's climbing over the rope."

"What's she doing?" Clyde asked. "She shouldn't go out there. It isn't safe."

"I hope she doesn't jump in the water. A guy leaped off the Tacoma Narrows Bridge a couple of months ago. Tried to kill himself and ended up paralyzed."

"She won't jump. It's a kid, showing off."

"Maybe it's a dare," his brother said. "The guy with her sees where she is. He doesn't seem concerned."

"He's old enough to know better," Clyde said. "I have half a mind to notify one of the ferry workers."

"Oh, don't get involved," James said. "We might have to stay and give a statement or something, and we'd be late getting home. My wife'll have a fit if I'm not there before her parents come to dinner."

"The girl is almost to the edge of the ferry."

"And we're almost to Bainbridge. The girl will come back on this side of the rope as soon as people start downstairs to get in their cars."

Clyde snuffed out his cigarette. "I suppose you're right," he said. "Let's go back inside."

Denny withdrew a short black gun, not much bigger than Matt's water pistol, and pointed it at Bonnie.

Bonnie stared at the gun. She didn't know what kind it was, only that it was aimed at her heart. A small gun could be just as deadly as a large one. Fear crashed against her like ocean waves.

Denny wouldn't get away with it; Bonnie was positive of that. As soon as Denny shot her, Matt would scream and run upstairs for help—and what would Denny do then? Shoot Matt, too? She shuddered.

Even if Matt got away and brought help and Denny was caught, it would be too late to save Bonnie.

She had to take action now, before Denny pulled the trigger.

Bonnie's mind flew in all directions, trying desperately to think of a workable plan. She glanced up again, but the two men had left; no one was watching.

"Keep going," Denny said. "Move!"

Bonnie lifted her left leg over the mesh rope and put her foot down on the other side. The edge of the ferry was only a couple of feet behind her. Trembling, she clung to the top of the mesh, one foot on either side.

Denny held the gun steady.

Over Denny's shoulder, Bonnie saw Matt move closer. His eyes showed his horror as he stared at the gun. He held the baseball against his chest.

Matt has a strong arm, Bonnie thought. He practices pitching all the time. Could he throw the ball hard enough and accurately enough to save her?

If he threw the ball at Denny and missed, Denny would be even more angry. He would shoot Bonnie instantly and then might turn the gun on Matt. Bonnie didn't want to endanger Matt to save her own life, yet she thought her idea could work. Matt was already in danger, and time was running out.

"You brought this on yourself," Denny said. "You always did talk too much."

"Zinger!" Bonnie yelled.

"What?" Denny said.

Matt froze. *Zinger* was the word he and Bonnie used for his hardest, fastest pitch.

Please, Matt, Bonnie thought. Please figure out what I'm asking you to do, and do it!

Bonnie lifted her right foot over the mesh rope. If she kept moving she hoped Denny would stay focused on her and not notice if Matt came closer.

"Zinger!" she shouted again. The wind lifted the word and carried it back toward Seattle, toward home and school and Mom. Bonnie wished the wind would pick her up, as well, and let her fly like a kite away from this cruel man and his lies.

She stood on the far side of the mesh now, gripping it with both hands. The wind was stronger out here, and the sea spray blew against her, dampening her hair and clothes. She tasted salt from the seawater on her lips. Or was it tears?

She looked straight at Matt and screamed, "Zinger!"

Matt understood Bonnie's message. Could he do it? With his heart racing, he gripped the Safeco Field souvenir ball in his hand. He saw the gun in Denny's hand but decided it was too small to be a good target.

Matt pretended he was in a ball game. The strike zone was Denny's back, and Matt knew he had only one chance; he couldn't miss.

"Good-bye, brat," Denny said.

Bonnie heard a click as Denny removed the safety catch. She stuck her left foot back, feeling for the deck, but she felt only empty space under her shoe.

She dropped to her knees and ducked her head, making herself into a smaller target. Hurry, Matt, she pleaded silently. Hurry!

Matt raised both arms over his head, his eyes focused on Denny's back. He gritted his teeth, lifted his left leg off the ground, and threw the baseball with every ounce of strength he had.

Thunk! The ball hit Denny hard, at the base of his neck.

Denny cried out in pain. He dropped the gun, fell to his knees, and clutched his neck with both hands. The gun landed on the deck and slid toward Bonnie.

Bonnie leaped over the mesh rope, rushed forward, and grabbed the gun. She turned toward the back of the ferry and flung the gun as hard as she could. It sailed over the mesh rope, far beyond the end of the boat, and splashed into the water.

"Run!" Bonnie yelled at Matt, but he was already halfway up the stairs, screaming for help.

Bonnie jumped over the yellow rope as Denny straightened up. He lunged for her and caught her by the ankle. She fell forward, getting slivers in her palms when she landed on the wooden deck. Bonnie kicked, struggling to get away from his grasp. His fingers dug in, bruising her skin.

With his weapon gone, she wasn't afraid of him any longer, and she fought with all her might, but he was too strong for her. He got to his feet, then grabbed her arms and yanked her upright.

"Help!" she shouted. "Help!"

Footsteps thundered down the stairs.

"That's him!" Matt yelled. "He has a gun!"

Denny clamped his hand across Bonnie's mouth and held her arms behind her so that it looked as if he still had the gun pressed to her back.

"Stop where you are," Denny said, "or the girl won't leave this boat alive."

The ferry workers and passengers who had followed Matt down the stairs stopped. For a moment no one moved or spoke.

"Who are you?" a man asked. "What do you want?"

Bonnie heard Denny's rapid breathing, smelled his fear, felt his fingers pressing against her lips.

"He's going to shoot her," Matt sobbed. "He's going to kill my sister!"

Bonnie forced her mouth open as wide as she could, then bit down hard on Denny's middle finger.

"Hey!" he said, and moved his hand just enough that Bonnie could speak.

"The gun's gone!" she yelled. "I threw it overboard!"

The adults surged forward, quickly overpowered Denny, and dragged him away from Bonnie. Two ferry workers pushed him facedown on the deck, then held his arms behind his back as the others reached for Bonnie.

Several voices spoke at once.

"Are you all right?"

"Did he hurt you?"

"Do you need a doctor?"

"I'm okay," she said, but her knees shook as she was led upstairs.

Bonnie and Matt were taken to a room marked PRIVATE. CREW ONLY. There they told the ferry captain and other workers what had happened.

The captain notified police on Bainbridge Island. "The police will board the ferry as soon as we dock," he told the children, "and take Denny Thurman into custody."

Next he let Bonnie call her mother.

"Hi, Mom," Bonnie said. "I'm okay, and so is Matt. We'll be home soon." Her mother, of course, had a hundred questions, so the conversation took a while. Then Matt wanted a turn to talk. By the time they finished, the ferry was docking.

No passengers or vehicles were allowed to leave until the police had boarded. A few minutes later Bonnie and Matt saw Denny get led to a waiting police car, his wrists handcuffed behind him.

Tears of relief trickled down Bonnie's cheeks as she watched. At last, the ordeal was over.

As the police car drove away, Matt said, "I always

thought it would be cool if my dad showed up, but it wasn't. I don't like him. He's a mean, rotten pickle-puss, and I wish I didn't have a dad."

Bonnie put an arm around Matt's shoulder. She'd spent years feeling cheated because her dad was gone, but she knew she was luckier than Matt. Her father was dead, but she had memories of a kind man, an honorable man who died a hero.

Matt would remember Denny.

Hard as it was to be without her dad, Bonnie still had pride in him. Matt would never have that.

"When you grow up," she told Matt, "you'll be a good man. You won't be anything like Denny."

"How do you know?"

"Because you're a good kid now. How you act is way more important than who your parents are."

"I'll act like Mom," Matt said, "and you."

A police boat docked next to the ferry, and two officers came aboard for Bonnie and Matt. "You get a private boat ride back to Seattle," one of them said. "It will be faster, and you can tell us what happened while we travel."

Officer Calvin met them in Seattle and drove them home while they told their story again.

A crowd of reporters and neighbors had gathered to welcome them. When Bonnie and Matt got out of the squad car, a cheer went up. Mrs. Sholter ran to greet them, followed by their grandparents, Detective Morrison, and Pookie. Pookie yipped and ran in circles around Matt.

Officer Calvin gave a statement to the reporters. Matt was declared a hero for bonking Denny with the baseball, and Bonnie was credited with being the brains behind the scheme.

Before they all went inside, Bonnie and Matt answered questions from the press and posed for more pictures.

One of the ferry workers had retrieved the Mariners ball for Matt, and he clutched it happily, demonstrating to the reporters exactly how he'd held it and how he wound up to throw his "zinger."

CHAPTER 23

Matt and Bonnie's safe return topped the news on every local channel Saturday night. Throughout the Northwest, television sets showed the missing boy and his sister reunited with their mother.

Bonnie, Matt, their mom, and their grandparents watched the reports together while they ate the macaroni-and-cheese that Stanley's dad had brought a week earlier. Mrs. Sholter had taken it out of the freezer as soon as she learned Matt and Bonnie were safe.

Pookie snoozed through the broadcast, even the part about him.

In a downtown apartment, Miss Clueless took off her banner, her red evening gown, and her high heels.

Wearing her comfy flannel bathrobe, she munched on salted peanuts as she turned on the TV.

Her jaw dropped in disbelief when she saw Denny in handcuffs being led from a squad car to the police station. That was the cranky man with the kids who had used the bathroom at the restaurant!

She stared at the TV screen, remembering how restless and angry the man had been, and how he'd rushed out of the restaurant when he learned his kids weren't in the bathroom.

A chill went up her arms as she recalled the red-haired woman who had reported the writing on the mirror. She had shrugged the woman off, positive the message was written by someone trying to send the other guests down the wrong path.

She tried to think exactly what the message had said. At the time she had only paid attention to removing it, not to the words themselves.

There had been names: Bonnie and Matt and Denny—the same names now being mentioned on the news.

Guilt spoiled Miss Clueless's appetite as she remembered her actions. She set down the dish of peanuts. Those poor children! They might have been killed because of her.

Across Lake Washington, a woman in Bellevue saw

the news, grabbed the phone, and dialed her friend. "Shelly!" she said, when the friend answered. "That girl in the bathroom who asked us to help her wasn't an actress!"

"What?" the friend said. "How do you know?"

"Turn on your TV," the woman said. "The girl had been abducted at gunpoint! Her brother, too!"

"You're kidding," said Shelly.

"I wish I were."

South of Seattle, in Kent, Eddie Gilden, the teenage driver who had stopped to talk to Bonnie and Matt, was eating lemon pie with his parents when he saw the reports.

Those kids in the street were telling the truth, Eddie realized. I could have saved them, but I drove off and left them with their kidnapper.

Eddie put down his fork, remembering how the girl had begged him to help. He and his pals had debated whether to look for a police officer and tell what had happened. "I don't think we should get involved," Eddie had said.

"Neither do I," the boy in back said. "That guy looked mean. He might remember your license plate and track you down."

"If he's mean," the third boy said, "maybe the girl

gave us the straight story. We should tell the cops about those kids and let them decide what to do."

In the end, the three boys drove home without disclosing the incident to anyone.

As he watched the news report, Eddie said nothing to his parents. He couldn't bring himself to call the other boys who had been in his car, to see if they'd seen the news. If he avoided them for a few days, maybe nobody would mention the two children who had pleaded for a ride.

The ticket seller at the ferry terminal was driving home from work when she heard the news on the radio. She gasped when she heard Bonnie's voice describing what had happened on the ferry. The girl said she'd tried to alert the ticket person, but the woman didn't understand.

That isn't true, the woman thought. I knew exactly what the girl meant, making her fingers into a pretend gun and all, but I didn't think it was for real.

She had watched the man and the two kids walk away; nothing in their manner seemed out of the ordinary. The man even put his arm around the girl's shoulder, like a loving father. She considered dialing 911, but then other customers came to buy tickets, and by the time she had a free moment again, she had convinced herself that the girl had merely been playing a joke. She never made the call.

With a lump in her throat, she listened to the rest of the radio report. Those children needed my help, she thought, and I turned away.

In their tidy home near Pine Lake, Ruth and Fred Faulkner cheered when they heard Matt and Bonnie were both safely home. They cheered again when the news coverage showed Matt running to his mother's arms. They cheered even louder when the camera zoomed in on Matt hugging Pookie.

"There's Monty!" Fred said.

"Oh, he looks so happy," Ruth said. "See how his tail is wagging? He's glad to see that boy again." She wiped tears from her cheeks.

Detective Morrison went off duty and got home in time to watch the ten o'clock news with her husband. She missed part of what Bonnie said because Spike, who was also off duty, kept playing with his loudest squeaky toy. Detective Morrison didn't mind. She'd heard it all in person and she figured Spike deserved some playtime.

One reporter interviewed the kidnapper's sister. Detective Morrison held Spike's toy so she could hear that part.

"I didn't know Denny had a child," Celia said. "He

never told me. He's mentally unstable and blames others for all his troubles. I've tried to get him into treatment, but he would never go. I apologize to the Sholter family for my brother's behavior."

"Apologies aren't going to be enough," Detective Morrison said. "The prosecutor will throw the book at Denny Thurman."

"Woof!" said Spike, and got his toy back.

The next afternoon, Mrs. Sholter baked three loaves of her special banana bread and took them to the police station where Detective Morrison and Officer Calvin worked.

"Here's a treat for all the officers who helped me get my children back safely," she said. She also took a large rawhide bone for Spike.

At two o'clock, the teachers from Jefferson School joyfully hit the streets, taking down the MATT IS MISSING posters.

Fred and Ruth Faulkner drove to the humane society Sunday afternoon. Faces aglow, they announced, "We're here to adopt a dog."

They didn't get one, though. They got two. When they found two older dogs who had lived together since they were puppies, Ruth and Fred couldn't bear to split them up.

"Old dogs are harder to place," a humane society worker told them. "Everyone wants a cute little puppy."

"Nothing wrong with getting old," Fred said.

"We'll each have a dog to walk," Ruth said. "It'll be good for our arthritis."

"That's right," Fred agreed, "and we'll never sit around getting bored with ourselves."

Matt and Bonnie spent Sunday afternoon playing cards with their grandparents and talking about their adventure to the many friends who called or stopped over.

"I shouldn't have believed Denny," Matt told Stanley. "Even after I saw Pookie in his car, I should have run back to class and told Mrs. Jules what Denny said."

"Bad guys lie," Stanley said.

"I should have screamed my head off," Matt said.

After the visitors left, Grandma and Grandpa decided to pack for their flight home the next day.

When Bonnie asked Matt if he wanted to practice his pitching, his smile would have lit up Safeco Field.

Bonnie crouched next to the garage and caught the balls Matt threw to her. After a few warm-up tosses, she called, "Give me a zinger!"

The two children grinned at each other. They both knew that for the rest of their lives, the word *zinger* would be a special bond between them.

How could I ever have wished for a sister instead of Matt? Bonnie wondered as the fastball streaked into her glove. She decided to buy him a "welcome home" present—a whole quart of strawberry ice cream, all for Matt.

On Monday in PE, Nancy said, "Last night I dreamed I jumped on a magical trampoline and bounced through a hole in the clouds. I think it means my life is dull and I'm searching for excitement."

"I think it means you should write fiction," Bonnie said. "Nobody has dreams like yours."

This time, talk of dreams didn't bother Bonnie. With her brother safe, she had slept soundly Saturday night and again Sunday night.

"Do you want to go to the mall with me and Sharon after school?" Nancy asked.

"I can't," Bonnie said. "Mom went back to work today, so I have to go home."

"Lucky you."

Yes, Bonnie thought. Lucky me. I get to ride the bus home with my brother, and pet Pookie, and catch the baseball while Matt practices his pitching.

She could hardly wait for two thirty-six.

PEG KEHRET is the author of many novels for young readers, including *Cages*, *Danger at the Fair*, *Horror at the Haunted House*, and *Earthquake Terror*. She lives with her husband, Carl, in the woods near Mount Rainier National Park in Washington State. Learn more about Peg Kehret at **www.pegkehret.com**.